The Soldier

ROBERT M WHITBEY

Small Town Hero Series Book #3

ISBN-13: 978-0692150429

ISBN-10: 0692150420

DEDICATION

To girls. You rock.

Preface

The Soldier took a while longer to write than my previous books. The reason is simple: Technology. I wanted to make sure the technology presented in the book was within the realm of possibility. I'm happy to say that it is. I won't spoil the story by getting into specific technological advancements, but I can say the average Joe or Jane is closer to being Bat-Man than ever before. 3D printing in your garage is scientific fact, not science fiction. AI that can interact and learn is happening now (Alexa is playing music SHE chose for me as I write this).

Another reason it took a little longer was that I have never personally been to Redmond, OR. Previously, I have always written about towns I had lived in, but I wanted to expand beyond my experience this time. I relied heavily on Google Maps and tried to use roads and landmarks that actually exist. For the record, I plan on a quick visit when time permits.

As usual, you do not need to read the previous books in the series to enjoy The Soldier. Astute readers, though, will find some Easter Eggs from past volumes. Epilogue #3 is based on events that happened in The Vessel. You might be a little lost on that one if you haven't read it, but please read it anyway. You'll be happy you did, I promise.

Prologue

Sargent Francine "Frankie" Connelly's eyes shot open. Staring intensely at the white ceiling tiles, she instinctively counted the number of tiny holes in each four-inch square. Each tile had a different number of holes. Within a few seconds, she had counted every hole on every tile.

As if her ears had suddenly switched on, she began to listen and recognized five different sounds. A heart monitor on her right beeping lazily. Presumably, it was her heart. An IV tube dripping regularly. She felt the cool liquid flowing into her arm. A squeaky wheel echoing as it rolled irregularly on the other side of a wall. A wheelchair, maybe? Male and female voices speaking just outside her open door. Medical personnel, based on their jargon. On the roof, far above, a helicopter was landing.

It felt as if her senses, her whole body, was waking up after a long nap. She began to flex her major muscle groups starting with her neck. There was no pain, but some definite stiffness. She spent several long minutes seemingly tracing her nervous system around her body, her nerves seeming to wake up and her muscles beginning to work.

When she had worked her way down to her feet and back up, she sat up in her bed. She looked from side to side and it was as she expected. This was a hospital room. Stateside, considering everything she heard or saw written was in English and the ambulance siren outside sounded normal.

Frankie turned to the edge of the bed and placed her feet firmly on the cold tile. She stood up straight and grabbed her IV bag off its perch. She walked, shakily at first, over to the open bathroom door. Stepping inside, she found a wall mirror. She sat her IV bag in the sink and slowly removed her hospital gown. She examined her body closely, scanning from the floor upward. She had lost a few pounds and her normally toned 'soldier muscles' had lost their fullness.

Her gaze finally reached her face. There she saw a large, spider-web of dark scars surrounding her left eye and spreading upwards over the top of her head. Her hair, which she normally wore just above shoulder length, so it could easily fit in the 'military bun,' was several inches longer than her shoulders. It was shorter around the scar tissue, but long enough that she had to brush her bangs back to see it. She used her index finger to trace the lines of the scar. They were deep but didn't appear to affect her vision. In fact, her vision seemed clearer than ever.

She put the gown back on and exited the bathroom. Walking over to the door, she removed her file from the clear plastic pocket above the light switch. As her eyes scanned over the paperwork, she read all the dates that had been written down. When she reached the beginning of the file, she found her date of transfer. She had been asleep in this hospital for over nine months. It was the last time Frankie would ever sleep.

Chapter 1

"Mornin', Clyde," said the tall, elderly man coming through the glass double doors of the thrift shop.

"Mornin', Ray," Clyde replied, from behind the cluttered front counter. "What brings you in today?"

The two gentlemen shook hands like old friends. Ray then produced a large plastic briefcase. Laying it on the counter, he opened the side. "I found this old portable phonograph in my garage. I don't think it works anymore. Do you think it's worth anything?"

"Whoa, buster! I haven't seen one of these in years! This is an Audiotrophic Solid State Phonograph. One went at auction last year for two thousand dollars. Of course, it was in perfect shape." Clyde fiddled with the dials with his thick fingers and appeared to be doing some quick calculations in his head. "I'll give you $800 for it. Or $1000 in store credit."

"For that old thing?" Ray questioned.

"Yeah," Clyde replied. "I'll get $1200 for the parts alone."

"I couldn't take that much, Clyde," Ray protested.

"Nonsense, I'm still making a huge profit." Clyde turned his head and called out, "Frankie, bring me $800 from the safe."

"Alright, daddy," came the feminine reply.

"Thanks, hon!" he called back. "Let's fill out the paperwork while we wait. I assume you want the money and not the store credit?"

"Y-Yeah," Ray said uneasily. The two men filled out the small form Clyde used to keep track of inventory. It also helped the police track down anyone that sold him stolen property. Since Ray was a long-time friend and customer, Clyde filled most of the form out from memory.

A few minutes later, a young woman came in with a bundle of money. "Hello, Mr. Tucker," she stated. She was medium height with an athletic build that was hard to see under her comfortable clothing. Most of her long brown hair was tied back except for a long, thin wisp that covered her left eye.

"Hello, Frankie," he replied, tipping his hat slightly. "How have you been, girl?"

"I am feeling very well this morning. Thank you for asking." She gave a short, quick smile and handed the money to Clyde, who was finishing up the paperwork. "Here you are, daddy."

"Thanks, hon. Could you take this phonograph to the back room?"

"I would be happy to." She folded it back up and carried it to the back of the store, disappearing behind some large appliances.

"She seems better. Less…. robotic," Ray said.

Clyde looked up from his paperwork as he finished. "She's learning to make facial expressions again. It's another step in her recovery." Clyde smiled with a glistening in his left eye. "She'll be back to her old self eventually."

Ray put his hand on Clyde's broad shoulder. "Of that, I have no doubt. She is a walkin', talkin' miracle already."

"That she is, that she is." Clyde had Ray sign the bottom of the form and handed him the money. "You tell that wife of yours we're still praying for her," he told Ray as they walked towards the door together.

"I'll do that, Clyde. Thanks for everything."

"And thank YOU for the phonograph. You just made my week." As Ray walked out the door, Clyde turned and saw Frankie standing by the front counter. He continued smiling as he walked toward her.

"I've never heard of an Audiotrophic Solid State Phonograph," she stated.

"That's because it doesn't exist. Ray is living on a fixed income and Belva has been in the hospital for weeks. From what you told me, the breast cancer is going to take her soon. Money should be the last thing he worries about right now. You know, Belva introduced your mom and me, God rest her soul."

"Still, you cannot afford to keep giving money away, daddy. Financially, we are sound for the time being, but you need to have something for your own retirement someday."

Clyde gently grabbed Frankie by her shoulders and stared into her eyes. "Frankie, my girl, I'll never retire. How could I leave all of this?" he said raising and waving his hands around. "And how could I live without seeing my little girl every day." He gave her a quick kiss on the forehead, then walked around the counter and took his seat to finish his morning paper.

Frankie turned and walked back into her office at the rear of the building. She spent most of her days there, feeling more comfortable by herself. She had been back home in Redmond for just under a year and people still looked at her in an odd way. It wasn't just the scars on her face, which were mostly hidden by her long hair and ever-present baseball cap. People could tell she was different by the way she acted.

Her office was her home away from home. Though it was small, it housed a great deal. One wall had six large touch-screen monitors all running to a single computer tower on the floor beneath her desk on another wall. Each monitor had something different on it. News websites, stock tickers, online auctions, and even a few camera feeds from around the building were all visible. The audio for each monitor was each at a different level. She had built much of the system from items found in the thrift shop. The temperature in her office was kept at a chilly 60°F because the computer got very hot at times. Her father never went inside because 'all that noise and light' gave him a headache.

Frankie's desk was immaculate. There was a separate computer system on it, rather old and clunky by her standards, but at least her dad could use it if needed. There was also a scanner that she used to input all paper transactions and a filing cabinet where those paper records ended up. She didn't need the filing cabinet, but, again, her dad might.

Another wall had a workbench with an assortment of tools and testing equipment and various electronic components. A few DVD players and flat screen TV's she recently fixed were stacked underneath it. A large trashcan next to the bench contained many discarded plastic pieces that used to house the electronic components now splayed on the bench.

Frankie stood before the monitors and 'absorbed' the information coming from them. She heard every sound and saw every part of every screen. She called this 'mainlining.' Every form of data available in her surroundings streamed into her brain and was filed away for her instant recollection. Everything she ever read, heard, smelled, tasted or felt was cataloged. She didn't even need to concentrate. It was happening whether she wanted it to or not.

She turned from the monitors when she saw her best friend Tim walk in the front door. She turned the volumes down and sat down at her desk, pretending to work. When he got to her open door, he stood there. His 6-foot 2-inch frame nearly filled the doorway. Smiling, he knocked on the pane.

"Knock, knock," he said.

Frankie turned to face him. She had a surprised look on her face and then a big smile appeared. "Why, Tim, I didn't hear you come in. How ARE you?"

Tim laughed. "That was almost believable," he coughed out. "But everyone notices when a large black man walks into the room."

"Especially when he's as handsome as YOU," Frankie gushed.

"Alright, alright. You don't have to spread it so thick. Eye contact and a small smile are enough for most people."

"I know, but you are SPECIAL."

"OK, ok, you're creeping me out now. Knock it off." Tim sat in the chair across from her. "Wait! Were you just trying to be funny? Was that a joke? That's great Frankie. Working on humor, again?"

Frankie's smile slipped away. "I am trying. I have over four million jokes in my brain but my poor delivery makes none of them funny. I miss humor. It may be the thing I miss the most."

Tim was the only person whom Frankie had confided the true depth of her physical changes. Everyone else, including her father, knew she had a traumatic brain injury and that it had 'stunted' her emotions. Only Tim knew what had really happened to her.

"Is that possible? For you to 'miss' something, I mean," he asked inquisitively.

"Yes, especially if it is something or someone I knew before the accident. It's as if my brain has holes in it. The nerve impulses moving around up there know there are holes they have to travel around and it 'bugs' them. Figuratively speaking, of course."

"I guess that makes some sense," Tim stated.

"Think of it this way. Remember that old house off I-97 that they tore down while we were deployed? Remember how you kept asking your dad what was different every time he drove you to your doctor's appointments in Bend?"

"Yeah, that was before the meds. I almost freaked out every time we got on the interstate until he figured it out. I forgot all about that."

"Precisely. Your brain knew something was missing and was bothering you to the point of triggering your anxiety disorder. Once you knew what was missing, you calmed down. But your brain still 'misses' the house, even though it was old and dilapidated and you had no real connection to it."

"I get it. Like when they put in a stop sign somewhere and you keep running it because your brain doesn't recognize it."

"That's not why YOU run stop signs," Frankie replied. Tim raised his eyebrows and nodded in submission.

"So, are people the same? Do you miss your mom?" Tim asked.

"Yes," Frankie said. "But not in a sorrowful way. I miss seeing her and my dad together. It doesn't seem right... to my brain."

"That's rough," Tim said morosely. The phrase was used often between the two since they were kids. "So, are we on for this weekend?" As he spoke, he slowly closed the door he sat next to.

"Absolutely. This week's destination is the Falling Thunder Casino outside of Mitchell. It's not huge, but we should easily be able to make ten thousand dollars without distressing the business."

"Awesome! I could use the cash. The VA is late with my check again."

Frankie reached toward her bottom drawer. "I have plenty of cash if you need it."

"Nope, Frankie, I have plenty for now. But next week I'm picking up a new rifle. Need the cash for that."

"Another rifle? How many do you need?"

"Ha, Ha," he replied sarcastically. "But this one is a beauty. Barrett 'fifty cal' in pristine condition. Serakoted in desert camo." As Tim spoke, he smiled big.

"The same one you used in Iraq."

"Yeah, but I'll need a better scope. The ones I have are not that good. A good scope costs more than the rifle."

"I can give you a bigger share if you like. It's not that big a deal," Frankie offered.

"Now, Frankie, we had a deal. You get 80%, I get 20%. In fact, I think I get too much. You do all the work. I just ride along to keep you company."

"And to be my backup if something goes wrong. Which has happened several times."

"Nothing you couldn't have handled on your own. Besides, all your gambling winnings keep this place going."

"True, our weekend excursions have proven to be very fruitful when coupled with the stock market." Frankie pointed to the monitor with the stock ticker rolling across. "My father's stock portfolio is currently worth $1,825,612.17 and will likely grow another 5% in the next week. When you combine that with the cash I keep stashed in various places, he's a very rich man."

"Are you ever going to tell him?"

"I have no plans to. I do all of our accounting and taxes. He just knows that when he writes a check or goes to the ATM, he has money in the bank. And the thrift store is a perfect cover for all of my large deposits."

"You're a genius, Frankie," Tim said as he rose to his feet.

"That is true," she replied.

"Well, 'Einstein,' how 'bout a beer tonight?"

15

"I'm busy tonight, but possibly tomorrow evening."

"Sounds good," Tim said. "See you then."

Frankie replied with a small grunt. She turned and began reading her monitors again as she turned their volumes back up. At the same time, she was reminded of all the time her and Tim had spent together. They had been friends since they were kids. Tim's father, who everyone referred to as Preacher John, was the preacher at her family's church. Since her parents were active members, the two had grown up together. While their parents had talked about them getting together one day, both Tim and Frankie knew there was nothing romantic between them. They were too much like siblings. Both had gone to college locally and they even joined the military at the same time.

Tim was injured in combat after Frankie. Six months into her coma, his unit came under attack while on patrol in a small Iraqi village. The ensuing firefight lasted two days due to a number of errors. Their position was miscommunicated to their base and their GPS locators had been shut off by the Iraqi Army soldiers that had turned on them. The helicopters that were finally sent to retrieve them accidentally opened fire on their position instead. When rescue finally took place, everyone in Tim's unit was dead. Only Tim, whose body was riddled with bullets, had survived. He spent months in rehab and only arrived back home a month before Frankie had.

Due to his injuries and PTSD, Tim was medically retired and given full disability. Emotionally, the medication he took kept him calm. Physically, he was in pain all the time. Though he did drink alcohol regularly, he would not take pain medicine because the pills 'dulled my mind too much.'

Frankie's day continued as normal. She had lunch at the counter with her father. He overpaid for several more items after lunch. The late afternoon rush was fruitful. At 6pm, her father told her to go home while he stayed another hour until closing time. It was their normal weekday routine.

On her way home, she stopped and picked up Chinese food for dinner. As usual, the owner jokingly remarked about how much food she was buying for just herself. She then drove her small SUV the three miles west of town to her home. The area outside of town was typical of that part of Oregon. Not many trees and lots of small hills.

The large house she called home was given to her by her uncle Pete. He owned a small junkyard with a house just outside the fence. No one had lived in it in decades. When she awoke from her coma, Pete visited her and saw how well she was doing physically. As they spoke, Frankie mentioned how everything in the hospital seemed loud and distracting and she was having trouble sleeping. Pete, who never married or had children of his own, returned and immediately had the entire home remodeled for her. At night, it was the quietest place around. He also remembered that Frankie and Tim used to play in the abandoned house when they were kids and hoped it would have fond memories for her. When she returned home, he gave her the keys and deed.

The farmhouse included a large metal shop building in the back. Outside, it was very well-maintained, a stark contrast with the junkyard next door with its tall chain-link fence and razor wire. But she didn't care about the aesthetics too much. Her home was where she could be herself and not have to pretend to be 'normal.'

She parked her SUV in front of the house, took the porch stairs two at a time and took her food inside through the front door. The living room was immaculate and decorated as you would expect a 19th-century farmhouse to look including period furniture. There was not a speck of dust anywhere.

She walked into the kitchen, turning on lights as she entered. It was also well-appointed with new appliances that looked like antiques. It was clean and orderly. She walked over to a large blender and began pouring the contents of the Chinese food boxes into it. Once the noodles, rice and meat dishes were all inside, she put the lid on and blended it to a very thin consistency. She then removed a large tumbler from the dish drainer and poured the liquefied Chinese food into it. Placing the lid and straw on top, she took a long pull from it. She was hungry. She drank a little more as she placed the empty boxes in the trash can.

Her tumbler with her, she walked up the stairs and down the hall to her room. As she opened the door, she clicked on the light switch and the room came to life. It was not a typical bedroom. There was no bed, only a recliner in the middle of the room. There were large flat panel monitors covering the largest wall. Some were tuned to regular television programming. Some showed constantly updating internet feeds of weather and stock prices.

"Good evening, Pippa," Frankie said aloud.

"I was wondering if you were going to say anything to me," came the snarky voice of a young woman from a small speaker in the corner.

"I'm still working on my manners, Pippa. You know that," Frankie replied.

"A woman with a perfect memory never forgets. You make choices," the voice pointed out.

"You're right. I apologize."

"Apology accepted. Should I cue up your normal feeds?"

"Please."

Frankie continued to her closet. The spacious walk-in closet held a large computer tower. The small room was noticeably cooler than the bedroom due to the small window air conditioner. Many colored cables ran across the walls. A small monitor near the tower displayed the environmental parameters of the room and the tower.

She stripped down and tossed her clothes into a hamper and took out her typical evening wear. For her, it was a gray sweatsuit, fresh socks and underwear and a camouflaged ball cap every night. She quickly showered and put the clothes on.

Taking a seat in the recliner, tumbler in hand, she stared at the screens. The volumes were much louder than in her office and each was set at a slightly different volume.

Frankie 'absorbed' the information from the monitors as she had done in her office. After two hours, she opened the armrest of the recliner and flipped a switch. The chair began to massage her back, legs, hips, and shoulders. It wasn't the most effective massage, but it worked well enough to keep her from getting too stiff.

Just after 11PM, she said aloud, "Pippa, I'm heading out to the shed. I'll stop and see Tommy first."

"Just like every night," Pippa replied.

Frankie stopped in the kitchen and pulled a small bag from the refrigerator. Outside, she walked across her side yard to a gate in the fence. A large, brown Rottweiler walked calmly towards her on the other side. She opened the combination lock and went inside, closing the gate behind her. The dog's mouth began to water as she withdrew a large, raw steak from the bag. She tossed it to his waiting maw and he ripped into it. Within seconds, he was licking his empty chops.

"Let's take a look around, Tommy," she told him. The dog followed as she walked around the junkyard. She had excellent vision even in the dark, but wore a pair of night vision goggles from the thrift shop. The junkyard wasn't very busy anymore since her uncle entered semi-retirement. He was only open a few hours each day and was usually fishing instead. If someone needed something, they would call him on his cell phone and he would tell them if he had it since his inventory system was in his head. If they wanted to drop something off, it was by appointment only. Still, each night Frankie would wander around with Tommy and look for any new items she could use. If she took something, she let her uncle know. But tonight, there was nothing new. By midnight, she was saying goodnight to Tommy and locking the gate.

Frankie walked over to a large metal shed behind her house. She unlocked the heavy metal side door using a keypad and went inside, the door automatically closing and locking behind her. Inside was spacious. One wall had a bank of monitors which came to life when she switched the lights on. None of them had their audio enabled, but each streamed dedicated information from the internet on their screens. There were several workbenches filled with various electronic devices in different stages of completion. In the middle of the room was something that resembled a motorcycle with its wheels turned horizontally. A large screen monitor hung from the rafters above the 'motorcycle.'

"Pippa, show me 'The Floaters' blueprints," she said out loud.

"Putting on-screen one," Pippa said.

The large monitor immediately showed the blueprints for the 'motorcycle' beneath it. On closer inspection, the object was not a motorcycle at all. Though the frame had originally been a 1970 Harley Davidson, everything but the frame pipes and handlebars had been removed. Where the engine had been contained an assortment of electronic boxes and wires of various colors. The front and rear horizontal 'tires' were not rubber tires at all. They were round copper hoops with coated wires all wrapped in zip ties. At the rear of the body, where the brake lights once sat were smaller versions of the coiled hoops. These two were different in that the coils protruded out a few inches, getting narrower and resembling two funnels. The large gas tank had been removed and a small tablet PC was mounted there instead.

Frankie used a stylus to draw a few changes on the schematic then grabbed a couple of small items from a workbench and walked around the bike to the back. She attached the items to the bike with zip ties and began installing them into the system of wires. When finished, she inspected her work, then took a thick cord off the wall and plugged it into a socket where one of the saddlebags used to hang. She then took another cord and did the same thing on the other side.

Taking a seat on the bike, she said, "Floater, on." The bike began to hum quietly as small colored LED's all over it began coming on in succession. The bike lifted slightly off its stand. The tablet blinked on showing the current environmental conditions for the bike as well as a host of other measurements currently being monitored. She placed her hands on the handlebars and gently turned them from side to side. As she did this, the hoops dipped slightly from side to side in unison.

"Pippa, begin recording to Notes. Entry #5,345. I installed the ceramic thermocouples as noted in my last entry. The power fluctuation issue has been resolved. I now estimate speeds in excess of one hundred miles per hour on flat ground if the batteries perform as stated. How far above that speed, I cannot determine without a proper test. As stated previously, terrain should not be an issue, however, travel over bodies of water may be slightly less responsive and not recommended at high speeds. I will be picking up the batteries at the post office in Bend on Saturday. Pippa, save to Notes."

"Saving to Notes," Pippa echoed.

"Pippa, are the batteries still shipping on time?"

"So far, so good. They left Atlanta at 2:33 AM yesterday morning. Should be at your secret PO box in Bend on Saturday by 10 AM."

"Don't call it a 'secret PO box.' It's just a regular PO box."

"Is the box registered to a fictitious company?" Pippa asked.

"Yes."

"Is your name attached to the box in any way?"

"No."

"Does anyone else know about it except you and I?"

"No, Pippa. You know that."

"Then, *ipso facto*, it's a secret."

"Fine. Just don't refer to it that way to anyone else."

"When do I talk to anyone else?"

"Other than internet chatrooms?" Frankie asked.

"That's for research," Pippa replied.

Frankie continued working on the bike for a few more hours, tightening belts and strengthening wire harnesses, as needed. Then she transitioned to her workbenches. She spent an hour at one bench and an hour at another working on smaller projects.

Pippa chimed, "I'm sure you are aware of this, but it is nearly 4AM."

"Thanks, Pippa."

She replaced her tools and cleaned up her workspace. She left the shop, shutting off the lights and equipment as she did. Although it was the middle of summer, it was cool outside and the sun was still an hour or so away. She took off the key from around her neck and went inside the front door, then up to her bedroom. Again, all of the monitors came to life as she stepped inside. She took her seat in the recliner and turned the massage on.

"Fire it up, Pippa."

"Done," Pippa replied. The screens hummed to life again. Frankie continued watching.

Her exercise routine began at 5:30AM. She put her running shoes on and exited the house. Her morning run was 5 miles through the hills in the growing light. She sprinted and slowed intermittently. Her muscles tightened as she got closer to home. Once she returned, she spent thirty minutes using the weight machine in the room next to her bedroom. She then showered and dressed.

"Ok, Pippa. Hold down the fort until I get home," she said as she walked towards the bedroom door.

"It's what I do," Pippa replied, a slight chuckle to her voice.

***

Gustavo Pacheco had killed his first man at the age of ten. It was part of his initiation into the Barrio Loco street gang. He didn't just kill the man, he tortured him for over eight hours first. Barrio Loco was known for its ruthlessness and if he wanted in, he had to show he was brutal.

That was almost forty years ago. Long before the Barrio Loco's were slowly killed or dispersed by the larger, even more ruthless South American gangs who took over Southern California. Now, he ran a small but successful drug operation based in Portland, Oregon. As he sat at a large table surrounded by his five captains, he was obviously not happy.

"I am tired, my brothers," he said shaking his head. He was always a big, muscular guy but had grown very fat in the last ten years. His captains weren't surprised he was tired. He often appeared tired and sweaty when they met.

"I am tired of living off the scraps," he said with some anger this time. He stood, his hands clenched. "These *vatos* from the south live large! They have killed so many of *nuestros hermanos*, yet all we do is scurry away like *ratos*!"

"But Tavo, what can we do?" asked the man closest to him. "They have killed so many of us over the years. There are not many of us *originales* left to fight."

"Listen to yourself talk! You sound like a woman, *cobarde*!" Gustavo walked around the table. The men watched him anxiously. He was on a tirade and when that happened, someone usually died. But this time, his face began to calm.

"The Southern gangs are strong only in number. But not where it counts. We both use fear, but they use it like a shotgun. We have always used it like a surgeon uses a scalpel. They are strong, but not smart. If they want to get to a judge, they kill his wife. That leads to either a compliant judge or a vengeful one. We kill his dog. More fear, less anger, always *obediente*, yes?"

The men all shook their heads in agreement. Many knew the specific instance Gustavo was talking about. Gustavo himself had nailed a judge's dog to a makeshift cross and left it in his chambers. It worked perfectly.

"Today, we begin rebuilding! It starts in here, where the Southern Gangs have no presence. We will move out to every town, no matter how big or small. Absorb or kill every small-time operator and, soon, we will take over all criminal activity across the whole state!"

The men began to mumble and talk among themselves. Then one man said, "Tavo, if anyone could do this, it is you. But we have limited ourselves to selling drugs for so long. What else do you have in mind?"

"Everything, *mis amigos*!" he shouted, throwing his hands up. "Drugs, theft, *proteccion*, sex trafficking, EVERYTHING!"

"But, Tavo, we know nothing of these other things," another man chimed in.

"I have arranged for some help. Consultants, that have more experience," Gustavo said.

"And they are willing to help us?" the bald man asked.

"Yes, for a piece of the action. It is easier to let us do all the work and they get part of the profit. When we have grown large enough, we cut them off or cut them down, eh?"

The men looked at each other, then all stood. The bald man stated, "We are with you, Tavo. Tell us what you want us to do."

"Let me show you what I've put together," Gustavo said, a deep smile forming on his lips.

Chapter 2

On Saturday morning, Frankie picked up Tim at 8AM. The drive to the Falling Thunder casino would take about an hour and a half. Frankie usually drove while Tim slept. This morning, however, Tim was awake for the entire ride.

"So, no late night?" Frankie asked.

"No," Tim said staring out the window. "I'm getting a little old for the Friday night booze-fest."

"Really?" Frankie asked.

"It's just not fun anymore," Tim explained. "Don't get me wrong, we both know I like a good time. But the bars are full of young people with skinny jeans and sculpted facial hair. How crazy is it that someone can dress like a lumberjack, yet still be feminine? Anyway, I feel like an old fogey around them."

"You're 28. That is hardly old," Frankie said.

"Yeah, but when you've seen the things we have, it ages you."

"I don't feel old."

"You don't feel anything," Tim replied. Almost immediately he continued, "Oh, heck, Frankie, I'm sorry. That sounded terrible."

"Don't worry about it," Frankie stated. "I can't get offended or sad." She smiled. "I could pretend if you want. Really give you the whole 'hysterical broad' thing."

"NO THANK YOU," Tim said. "Good smile, by the way."

"Thanks. Please continue with your story, Old Timer."

"I don't want to get too morose, you know. It's just that sometimes I think about my buddies, the ones I lost, and I think of what a waste it is for me to be sitting in a bar, flirting with a girl that's out of my league, getting drunker by the minute. I should be doing something, I don't know, MORE."

"I understand. I felt something similar. You're not the same person. Somehow, you think the trauma should have made you a better person. Your life should have more meaning because of those that died with you."

"Exactly! Like I'm not honoring their sacrifice or something. So, how did you get through it?"

"I hacked into computers all around the world and used the data to build a hoverbike."

"Come on, Frankie. I mean really, what did you do?"

"It may sound silly, but I concentrated on my dad. He's worked hard his entire life to build a future for his family. He supports his community to a fault. He's an incredible human being. I decided I would do whatever I could to support him in his endeavors. It won't bring about world peace, but it will allow him to live in a way that makes him happy and fulfilled. I find sound logic in that."

"That's beautiful, Frankie. And you're right, Clyde is an incredible dude. When our moms died, he held it together a lot better than my dad did. It took him months to come around. Your dad was a rock for us all."

"It didn't take long for Preacher John to step up."

"He was a mess for a while, but eventually he worked through it. I'm sure it was guilt more than anything. They were only at the church building alone because he forgot to meet them there. He was making visits at the retirement home when they got killed." Tim stopped talking for a minute, his voice caught in his throat. "I still remember when he came home. Vacant look in his eyes. You know, your dad was the first to even hug me? I stayed at your house most of the time until dad came around. Clyde was a real hero."

"I doubt he would agree. Everyone just copes with loss in their own way."

They drove for a few more minutes before Tim asked, "You ever miss it? Being a hero, I mean?"

"I never really felt like a hero, to be truthful. But I was rarely in the thick of things like you were. I didn't deal with the civilians much, either. I just told soldiers where to go most of the time. It was just dumb luck that had me in that Humvee when we hit that IED. Our mission was over, for the most part. I'm just glad I was the only one seriously injured."

"When we drove off the bad guys, or killed them, the civilians, most of them, loved you. They threw flowers at our feet. They were so happy. Sure, some hated us, but most of them loved us. It felt good to be the hero. I miss it."

"So, go to the police academy. You talked about it before we went in."

"They would never take me. Between the PTSD meds and the shape my body is in, I would never qualify."

"How about teaching self-defense? You were always a good instructor."

"Yeah, I could do that again. It might do some good. Great idea, Frankie. Beats sitting around the house."

"Or you could always go into preaching, like your dad."

"Nah, I never liked public speaking. Plus, there are personal expectations I could never live up to."

"Like, no flirting at bars with girls that are out of your league?"

"Exactly."

They soon saw the sign for the Falling Thunder casino and exited the highway. It was not much to look at. The casino was a large steel building with a small parking lot. Inside, was Las Vegas-inspired flash. Lots of neon. Lots of flashing lights. Gold-accented everything. They had card tables, dice games and lots of different slot machines. Being a Saturday morning, it wasn't too busy yet, but there were enough players that the two newest visitors wouldn't stick out.

Their game was simple. Frankie would spend time at each table and Tim would spend his time playing the slot machines nearby. He had nearly $100 in quarters rolled up in a small messenger bag he carried. Frankie would try and space out her winnings throughout the day. If it looked like management was eyeballing Frankie too much, Tim would come get her and they would leave. He always carried a handgun concealed in his waistband just in case he needed it. He had never drawn it so far.

Frankie bought $100 in casino chips. She began by playing Twenty-One. She could have won nearly every game, but was sure to lose a few every now and then. She then moved on to the poker tables. Again, she could have won a lot more often, but didn't want to arise any suspicion. Every $1000 in winnings would be placed in her purse so she didn't have to openly carry around a large amount of chips. By 3PM, she had reached her goal of $10,000. She excused herself and went to turn in her chips.

Tim was watching nearby and as she filled out her tax forms, he left the casino. Frankie requested a cash payment and left the building, too. Outside, they walked to her SUV together. Tim keeping his 'head on a swivel.'

As they neared the car, two men exited the large car on their passenger side. Both were dressed in nice suits with one slightly taller than the other. Both were of obvious Native American descent.

"Can I have a word with you, ma'am?" the taller man asked.

"We're actually in a hurry," Tim said, waving them off.

"This won't take but a minute," the taller man replied. The shorter one was walking to intercept Tim.

"What is this about?" Frankie asked.

"You won a substantial amount of money. We would like to know how," the tall guy asked, moving towards Frankie slowly.

"She's good at card games," Tim stated. "Nothing wrong with that."

"No, nothing wrong with that unless you were being assisted by someone else," the shorter man replied, looking straight at Tim.

"You got us. I'm the eye candy she uses to throw everyone off their game," Tim said sarcastically.

"We would like you to come inside and wait while we review the camera footage. To make sure you were not being assisted in any way," the taller man said to Frankie.

"You have her name and address on the tax forms. If you suspect anything, have the sheriff pay her a visit," Tim suggested, knowing the address she gave was a PO Box.

"It will only take a few minutes," the taller man said, reaching out to Frankie.

Tim suddenly gave a sharp upward elbow strike to the shorter man, whose nose erupted in a shower of blood. Tim quickly followed that up with a spin that struck the man on the back of the knees, collapsing him to the ground.

The taller man spun towards Tim, pulling a revolver from a shoulder holster. Frankie's fist was a blur as it struck the man under the arm, causing it to go limp. His hand released the revolver as his arm dropped to his side. Tim grabbed the gun and turned, kicking the man under the jaw. Both men were rolling on the ground as Frankie's SUV quickly left the parking lot.

"Woo boy! What a rush!" Tim yelled.

"We may have been better off just going with them," Frankie stated.

"You know as well as I do that if we went with them, we weren't coming out any time soon. They would look for any loophole possible to keep us there. As long as we're on this reservation, they hold all the cards."

"I agree, but you didn't wait for him to touch me. I had my cell phone recording the encounter from my pocket. If he had put a finger on either one of us, we were justified in our response. But you struck before he actually touched me. Now our defense is more in a gray area."

"Frankie, those two aren't going to report this. For one, it was on the reservation and the reservation police have no jurisdiction off the reservation. Second, nothing on the video from the casino will implicate us in any wrongdoing. Third, the big one just got beat up by a girl."

"I'm not saying they will do anything, just that our defense is a lot easier if they actually touched us. And if they thought they could retrieve their $10,000, they might try to press charges."

"$11,000," Tim corrected.

"I won exactly $10,000, Tim."

"I know, but I won $1,000 on the quarter slots," Tim smiled.

***

Gustavo stood at the head of the table while the rest of the gang leaders sat. The room was thick with smoke from cigarettes, cigars and hash. The warehouse that served as Gustavo's headquarters had a vivid view of the Portland Skyline as well as the docks along the Colombia River.

"So, *amigos*, it is good to see you all again so soon," Gustavo began.

The assembled men replied with smiles and gestures. All were smart enough not to speak until spoken to. This was the norm in the meetings of Barrio Loco. Talking out of turn might mean one less person for drinks afterward depending on Gustavo's mood.

"All of you have served our organization well for many years. At our last meeting, I told you of my bold plan to put us back at the top. Now we are ready to begin. The man sitting to my right is Mr. Aliwall. He has been employed by many overseas organizations over the years. He specializes in, well, what would you say, *mi amigo?*"

"Making money for my friends," the small Arab man with thick glasses replied with a smile. His voice bore no distinct accent.

Gustavo laughed loudly, "Yes, yes. Mr. Aliwall has many 'friends' he has made very wealthy. On my left is Mr. Beloch." Gustavo pointed to a very large bald man with deep scars on his face. "I could tell you what he does best, but then I would have to kill you all!" The men broke out in raucous laughter. Mr. Beloch did not crack a smile.

"With the help of these 'consultants', we will soon take over all organized action in this state. Then, we move on to others. Mr. Aliwall has outlined exactly what steps will be taken and when they will happen. Mr. Beloch will see to it that those steps are carried out."

Gustavo's face turned serious as he took a deep breath. He put both hands on the table and looked at the men around it. "You will follow the orders of these two men like you follow mine," he stated with a threatening lilt to his voice.

Chapter 3

Frankie stood back and admired her work. The new batteries fit perfectly in place of the saddlebags on The Floater, although they were about two feet taller. She had picked up all four batteries from her PO Box in Bend after their casino visit and had begun topping off their charge as soon as she got home. By 9PM, they were at their full capacity and ten minutes later, she had installed two of them, leaving the other two as spares.

The batteries were the newest technology available and were very expensive. Each one can power an entire home for several days when fully charged. The claims by the manufacturer were apparently well-founded. Her small creation now hovered two feet above the ground, the hoops humming gently.

The blue LED lights that dotted the bike allowed her to monitor systems without having to watch the large tablet installed in place of the gas tank, which would require you to be sitting on it to view. Plus, she had to admit, they made her ride look pretty sharp. She circled The Floater, intently staring at the many small systems integrated into it.

"Pippa," she said, "begin recording to 'Notes.' Audio and video. Entry #5,346. The batteries have been installed and are working optimally. The Floater is staying true to its name currently hovering approximately two feet above the ground." She climbed on the bike and it did not move. "Hover is stable at that height when I am on it. There is no lateral movement. Hoops are perfectly balanced." She stood on the foot pegs and jumped a few times. "There is a slight downward motion as I jumped up and down which will be good for shock absorption. Executing hairpin spin now."

Frankie planted her left foot on the ground and used her body weight to spin the bike around. "Hairpin took only a small effort to accomplish. I'm a little worried about how true it will ride in a cross-wind. The bike weighs 793 pounds but feels almost weightless to push. Pippa, pause notation."

Frankie stepped off the bike and walked over to her workbench. She lifted a pink bicycle helmet covered with large sunflowers and placed it on her head, securing the chin strap. She then grabbed a pair of large plastic goggles and put them on.

"That's so cute," Pippa said sarcastically.

"Yeah, yeah. What's the ETA on the helmet?"

"Tracking update as of today at 2:15PM shows you can expect it by 8PM Thursday."

"Excellent. Resume notation. The heads-up display has not been completed as of today, so I will be using a standard bicycle helmet and the onboard tablet to monitor the systems. As a reminder, the heads-up display will incorporate a helmet with augmented reality currently being built by Plobias Systems. It is crude and will no doubt require much modification on arrival, but the base components are sound and obtaining this functional yet prototypical equipment will save me a minimum of forty hours of build time and at least $20,000 in tools and supplies. The $2,000 price tag is well worth it. I have ordered three working models at this point."

Frankie grabbed a small camera from another workbench and attached it to the helmet, powering it up. She quickly put on a pair of thick coveralls along with knee pads and elbow pads. She took off her comfortable sneakers and exchanged them for heavy boots that allowed her to tuck-in the long legs of the coveralls. She knew she looked ridiculous, but she was also unrecognizable and these clothes improved her safety far more than her normal evening attire. She sat on the bike and snapped on a four-point harness that kept her firmly planted in her seat.

"Pippa, transfer all recording responsibilities to The Floater and Helmet Cam #1. And please stay connected for voice protocols." A couple of beeping sounds were audible on the bike.

"Done, Chief. Looks like I get to go for a ride. And, for the record, I still think you need to change the name."

"Noted. I'll start slow, around the yard and throttle up when I get to the road. Continue recording until I tell you otherwise."

Frankie slowly rotated the throttle on the right handlebar. The Floater began to edge forward. She twisted the handlebar as she exited the main shop door and the Floater responded in kind. She increased the speed a little more and began to do a slow figure eight in her backyard. She then used her row of rose bushes like traffic cones, zig-zagging around them, increasing her speed until she flattened one of the bushes. Then she turned toward the road.

"The handling is far better than I expected. Despite my fears, there is no detectable drift sideways. Of course, in a stronger wind, it might be worse. I'm heading to the main road for speed checks."

Frankie moved onto the pavement. She rarely saw any cars driving out here at night, but checked before she entered anyway. The night was very dark and now she was far from the exterior lighting of her property. The Floater's many LED's were even brighter now. She tapped a button on the tablet and her front headlight illuminated her path. It was an upgrade from the stock headlight that was on the frame when she found it. The beam was wider and brighter than normal, but she could control either parameter.

One last scan of the tablet showed her that all systems were nominal. She slowly increased speed. The stretch of road leading away from town was nearly ten miles long with only a handful of homes before it dead-ended into a crossroad. It was straight mostly, with only a slight bend to the right at mile seven. The speed limit was seventy miles per hour although most people in this rural area did at least eighty.

The Floater zipped along a bright beacon in the night. At one hundred miles per hour, she reached the slight bend. She leaned to the right as she turned the handlebars accordingly and then straightened it back out. She gunned it and before long she had reached one hundred and forty miles per hour. She knew she could go faster, but she wanted at least a mile to slow and turn around. She eased off the throttle until she was moving slow enough to turn around.

"Pippa, is the audio-level OK?"

"Affirmative," she heard from a speaker on the tablet.

"Good. As you can see from the recording, I managed to achieve one hundred and forty miles per hour. I think I can hit two hundred under the right conditions. A few problems of note. Number one, the lack of an engine pitch change when speed increases would likely be disorienting to most people at night. Perhaps adding a light bar that increases with speed would help. Number two, wind noise is very bad at speeds above eighty miles per hour. A full helmet that covers the ears is recommended, although headphones would probably work, too. I will complete a full system check back at the shop."

Frankie began to throttle up as she headed towards her home. She glanced at the time on the tablet. It was nearly 2AM, just as her internal clock told her. She didn't really need a clock anymore, but old habits die hard.

Suddenly there was a flash of white light in her eyes. Knowing its meaning, she quickly yelled, "Pippa, auto-drive! Take me home!" Then the pain began to grow from the middle of her head and radiated outward as it had thirty-three times before. A blinding searing pain that took away every other sensation. Only the harness around her waist kept her in her seat as she slumped and grabbed at her head. Her whole body shook violently as she was racked with pain. She had no idea what was going on around her as she could think of nothing but the excruciating pain in her head.

Then just as suddenly as it started, the pain went away. Straightening up in her seat and she took stock of her surroundings. She was in the shed, the large door closed behind her. She removed the helmet and wiped her face with her glove. She fumbled with the harness until it unlatched and half-stepped, half-fell off the side.

She stumbled over to a small door and opened it exposing a tiny bathroom. Though the worst of the pain was gone, she was still very groggy and her head felt like a muscle recovering from a deep cramp. She removed her clothes which were covered in urine, vomit, and blood from her nose and washed her face. She used the same small towel to do a quick wash of her body, then put on a pair of baggy shorts and a t-shirt that had been placed there for emergencies. A water bottle sitting on the counter was quickly drained and Frankie could feel her mind beginning to focus. The reduced pain in her head would be there for days, but it would slowly subside.

As Frankie walked back into the main shop, she looked at the large monitor and saw the time. Nearly 3AM. She was out of it for almost an hour this time.

"Thanks for getting me home, Pippa."

"No problem, Chief. Was it worse this time?" Her voice was filled with concern.

"Maybe a little. It's hard to say. Let's see what happened. Begin playback of last entry at 1:58AM, triple speed."

"On screen one."

Frankie watched as the events of the last hour played out. There were five cameras on The Floater as well as her helmet camera.

The audio from three sources also played. She watched as her limp body was shuttled back to the shop at low speeds, taking the exact same route as she took to get there, including the zig-zagging around her rose bushes, the figure eights in her backyard and the hairpin turn in the shop. She also watched as she sat in the shed, paralyzed in pain.

"Well, the Auto-Drive and Return-Drive worked perfectly. I was able to activate both features vocally before it incapacitated me. I'm going to add a feature so that Pippa can monitor my vital signs and return me home automatically should I become incapacitated. I was lucky it didn't come on faster. Somebody might have come along and stumbled on my little experiment. Tomorrow night, I will do some test runs over varying terrains as planned. Save to Notes."

"Done. You know, I would have brought you back anyway. I could tell you were in trouble."

"I appreciate that, Pippa. Your abilities are progressing even faster than I had anticipated. However, you may need to someday summon an ambulance for me. I would like to program you with the ability to discern its necessity."

"Good idea, Chief."

"And stop calling me Chief!"

"You got it, Chief," Pippa responded with a chuckle.

Frankie began to clean up the shop, though it wasn't in real disarray. She attached a cable to The Floater and tapped an icon on the main monitor to start the full diagnostic of the bike, which would take several hours. She placed the helmet camera back on its charger and put the old bike helmet on a peg in the wall. Once she was ready to leave, she stopped and turned to face the room.

"Pippa, open Medical Notes."

"Go ahead."

"Entry #59. I had another pain episode at 2AM this morning. I was riding my experimental motorcycle when it came upon me. I didn't crash due to precautions I had taken. The episode lasted nearly an hour and, as usual, it completely incapacitated me the entire time. I have a small headache now, pain level 5, but all other faculties are back to normal. I continue to be perplexed by them. Why can I control every other sensation my body experiences except this one? Still, no common trigger and the time between episodes as well as their duration remains completely random. Pippa, save to Medical Notes."

Frankie closed up her shed and went back inside the house. The pain in her head was already lessening, but she decided to forego her usual sensory input during her morning massage and opted to just focus on a few sitcoms. From experience, mindless television helped the pain in her head to subside more quickly. She had tried not watching anything after a pain episode a few months back and, oddly enough, it seemed to make the pain last longer. So she settled into her massage chair and watched several episodes of the *Andy Griffith Show* at the same time.

***

Pedro and Wally weren't happy with their assignment. As they drove through the mountains on their way to Bend, OR, both had a sneer on their face. They were both 'city boys' and hated small towns. But Tavo had personally ordered them and the other groups to go to the middle of nowhere and 'set up shop' and that is what they were going to do.

Their orders were to lay low and scope out the local competition for a week or so. Once they knew who was running things, either bring them on board or kill them and bring their own people in. According to Mr. Aliwall, it was better to use the locals.

There were 'not a lot of Hispanics in the area,' so most of their group would stick out.

Pedro, the brains, and Wally, the brawn, were sure they could get the locals to work for them. Both were chosen, in part, for their ability to blend in with the local *gringos*. But both men were also ruthless in their work. They 'got stuff done.'

Similar two-man groups had been dispatched to other small towns around Oregon. Their targets were towns with populations under 75,000 that were surrounded by smaller towns. They would start in the larger areas then expand to the smaller. Within a year, they would be running the entire state, according to Mr. Aliwall.

Chapter 4

A few days after her test run, Frankie sat at the front desk while her father was at an early lunch with friends. It was hard for her to sit with nothing to do, so she had three separate tablet PCs sitting on the table in front of her streaming financial market data, an episode of *Mythbusters,* and a soap opera.

A young woman walked in the door carrying a large cardboard tube. She was in her late-20's, middle eastern, but definitely westernized. Frankie didn't know her, which was surprising considering she knew everyone in Redmond.

"Good morning. How can I help you?" Frankie asked.

"Good morning," the young woman said with no detectable accent. "I picked up this print recently at an estate sale and I was on my way back to Portland. The waitress at the diner down the street, Becky was her name I think, she told me that you guys can appraise artwork."

"Sure, ma'am, I can help you with that."

"Fantastic!" she said, removing the rolled print from the tube.

They flattened the print out on the counter and Frankie examined it. It was paper but obviously very old. The picture was made up of geometric lines and cubes.

"The print is obviously very old, but I'm not sure how old. More than two hundred years, though. It's not canvas, but likely some type of textile and paper. I'm not sure who the artist is. It has both Impressionist and Cubist tendencies. It reminds me of some of the artwork in an old book called the Voynich Manuscript. It's rumored to be from the fifteenth century, but no one really knows what it is. Maybe this print is connected to that in some way."

"Interesting," the young lady stated, staring at Frankie.

"It really is interesting," Frankie repeated. "I wish I could give you a value, but it's unlike any artwork I'm familiar with. It's probably priceless, though, based on the age alone. Someone obviously took good care of it for many years."

They gently rolled the print up and placed it into the tube. The young woman smiled at Frankie the whole time. "Thank you very much for your time. I'll look into it more when I get home."

"No problem. It was my pleasure," Frankie replied with a wave as the young woman exited the door.

Frankie had noticed a man outside the front doors, who had passed by several times. He was approximately six feet tall, 170 pounds, possibly mid to late twenties. Though he was dressed in civilian clothes, she was sure he was military. Given the sharpness of his haircut, he was likely still active duty. As soon as she saw his face, she knew exactly who he was.

The man entered the two doors hesitantly and looked around. Though the desk counter was in plain sight, people often missed it at first glance due to the enormous amount of goods for sale. When he spotted the girl behind the counter, he made a beeline towards her. The smile on his face got wider as he approached.

When he got within ten feet, Frankie suddenly stood at attention. The move startled the man, stopping him in his tracks. He quickly recovered.

The man stepped forward to the counter and said, "At ease, soldier." Frankie relaxed but still stood. The man smiled and asked, "What gave it away?"

Frankie looked at him and replied, "Your walk initially, but the hair affirmed my speculation."

"And how did you know I was a superior officer?" he asked.

"Your hands, Sir. The hands of a surgeon. Likely a Major."

"That's very good, Sargent. I'm Major Lawrence Spence. I'm sure you don't remember me, but I was the trauma surgeon who initially worked on you after your injury."

Frankie knew exactly who he was. She had researched everything she could about her case including records normally protected. She wasn't going to give too much away, though.

"It's very nice to meet you, Sir," she said sticking her hand out. They shook cordially, their eyes never breaking each other's gaze. "What brings you to beautiful Redmond, Oregon?"

"You, not to put too fine a point on it. I've been state-side for a few weeks visiting my dad in Colorado. I had a few days left to report back and I really wanted to check up on you, believe it or not."

"That's a long house call," she said, then threw in a small smile.

"I know it sounds crazy, but you were a 'special' case. I wasn't able to get access to your records until recently and I wanted to meet you and see how you were progressing. To see if there was anything I could still help with."

"You do this with all of your patients, Major?" she asked suspiciously.

"One or two. Cases that are special, like yours."

"Special in what way?" she asked.

"Well, you should be brain-dead, for one. But your records from Walter Reed show your cognitive abilities have significantly increased as has your sensory awareness. As I recall you've had some emotional issues and you had trouble sleeping, and migraines from time to time. Is that accurate?"

"Sounds about right, Major. Are you thinking of treating me? I do have a family physician that is doing a fine job."

"I'm sure he is, but, as I said, you were a special case. I'd like to talk to you about it a little more in depth. Would it be possible to go someplace a little more private?"

"Unfortunately, I can't leave the store unattended." Frankie thought about it for a second. This man was the first to treat her after her accident and he seemed especially committed for some reason. Most of her past doctors were not so attentive. He may have some answers for her. "Would you be willing to come by my home tonight for dinner? Say seven o'clock? You saved my life, so I at least owe you a dinner."

"I think that would be perfect."

Frankie jotted down her address and handed it to the Major. She also gave him a rough idea of how to get there verbally and he took notes. They shook hands again and the Major left the building.

The afternoon passed more slowly than usual for Frankie. She debated with herself on the merits of telling the Major everything or only revealing small bits of information. Was it possible he could help cure her brain trauma? Could she be normal again? Did she even want to be? At this point, she knew as much about the brain as most top neurosurgeons and didn't think she could be treated.

Still, there was much she didn't know about her own condition. She knew there were metal fragments embedded in her brain tissue that prevented an MRI from being done. And CT scans only showed the metal was there, but not much else. Could a trauma doctor do for her what others failed to do? The chances weren't good, she decided.

By 6PM she was leaving the store. She stopped and picked up her regular order of Chinese take-out doubled for her dinner guest. She found herself still running through possible scenarios. The uncertainty was actually kind of nice, she thought.

When she got home, she immediately went through her downstairs area making it look as 'normal' as possible. She dusted areas and fluffed up the couch. She got plates and cups and silverware out and washed them. She put music on her Bluetooth speaker. When finished, she quickly showered and got dressed. As she looked in the mirror, she contemplated whether or not to put on makeup. She hadn't worn any in months, but her instinct was to try and cover her scar. She wondered why it even occurred to her to do it. After all, this wasn't a date. It was a doctor's appointment with refreshments. In the end, she did not wear any makeup but did wear her hair down.

The Major arrived just before seven. She answered the door and they exchanged pleasantries, then moved to the small kitchen where the food was laid out. As they began, the Major said a short silent prayer then began to eat quickly, as he was trained to do, then slowed when he saw Frankie studying him.

"Sorry," he said.

"It's no problem, Major. Soldiers are trained to 'eat now and taste it later.' It takes time to get used to civilian life. How long have you been in, if I may ask?"

"Eight years or so, since I finished residency. Most of that has been in The Sand Box. And please, call me Larry. I've never been one for formality."

"Only if you call me Frankie," she replied. "Eight years after residency? How old are you, Larry?"

"Thirty-six."

"You don't look it."

"I get that a lot."

"Eight years is a long time for a doctor to stay active duty. Usually, they stay in the service only as long as they have to, then return home and make the big bucks. Any reason why you stayed?"

"I like what I do," he replied. "You're right, not many long-term doctors in the service anymore. But I consider it a sacred duty to help soldiers. The longer I stay, the better I get at it. But I have to admit, I am getting somewhat fatigued by it all. Something happened recently that has me re-examining my life. I've been back in The States for a few weeks now, getting re-acclimated. I think I may just sit out for a while."

"You said earlier you were visiting your father. Is that the only family you have?"

"Yeah, we lost my mother some time ago. Car accident. No brothers or sisters. Just me and dad. But enough about me. I want to know about you. I have spent a lot of time looking at your military medical records and they are fascinating. Have there been any significant changes since you were discharged?"

"I think I'm still adjusting, physically and mentally. When I finally came home, it was like everything was familiar, but changed. I seem to notice more if that makes any sense."

"Can you elaborate?" Larry asked, taking a final scoop of noodles into his mouth.

"Well, I think it's a matter of how one views their surroundings. It's almost like I'm observing everything from multiple perspectives. And not just seeing things that way, but experiencing all my senses at the same time. And not forgetting any of it."

"I'm sorry? Not forgetting any of it? Like, ever?" Larry stared hard at her and Frankie self-consciously looked down. Sensing her unease, Larry smiled and asked, "Are you saying you remember everything you experience?"

Frankie thought for a moment, then spoke up. "Larry, I would like to share with you what has happened to me, but I would like to keep it between us. I don't want it as part of my Army medical records. Can you agree to that?"

Larry wiped his mouth and put his napkin on his plate. "As I told you, Frankie, I'm here as your doctor, not as a soldier. I want to assess your current situation and, if possible, offer you some relief. I will keep your secrets if you will agree to keep mine."

"Your secrets?"

Larry stood. "Do you agree to the terms?" He stuck out his hand.

Frankie thought for a moment, then replied, "I agree." She shook his hand.

"Then allow me to go first." Larry picked up a steak knife from the table, held his wrist over the empty plate and cut it deeply. The blood that flowed was very dark red, indicating he had hit an artery. Frankie did not gasp as he had expected, but her eyes did narrow as the flow of blood began to cease almost immediately. Within a few seconds, it had stopped completely and there was no sign the skin had been severed.

"My parents always knew about it. Not to be crude, but my parents first realized something was wrong when I was circumcised twice. My dad watched the first time and just after the doctor walked out of the room, the skin grew back. When he came back into the room, he was sure he had done it, but looking at me figured he must not have. He repeated it and, again, walked out of the room. My dad watched it grow back both times. He knew something was up and got me out of the building before anyone could notice."

"Fascinating," Frankie observed. "Does the amount of damage matter?"

49

"Well, I've been in a major car accident, the one that killed my mother. I've had some pretty bad trauma, but always recovered quickly. I imagine that is why I look so young, too. But that's only part of it. When I was a teenager, my dad accidentally backed over our family dog. I was the first one to grab him. I loved that dog. He was as old as I was. I hugged him close and cried. Then, he was fine. He had been completely healed. He jumped out of my arms and took off running toward the house. In fact, he was in better health than before. He lived another ten years before he died of old age."

"Incredible. I'm assuming that is how you helped me?"

"Exactly, through a lot of practice, I have been able to determine what is wrong with someone and to heal people in a very specific way just by touching them. I can heal a broken bone without healing the wound the bone made as it protruded through the skin. I can take away lung cancer without regenerating a new lung. As you can imagine, I try to keep it as under the radar as much as possible. My only personal limitation is I won't bring anyone back to life. If they flat line, I'll do everything humanly possible to save them, but I won't use my abilities."

"But why put that limitation on yourself? Surely, all lives are worth saving."

"Most are, yeah, but I have to believe that some people are meant to die. I'll give you an example. The first person I brought back several years later ended up being the drunk driver that killed my mother. Now, that had to be a sign from God himself, don'tcha think?"

"I'm not sure I believe in God," Frankie said abruptly.

"Trust me, I've had my moments, too. But I'm still a Believer."

"So, I wouldn't have died?" she asked.

"You were in a bad way, but you probably would have survived in a vegetative state. I healed much of your wounds, even the outward ones because very few people had seen you. Your brain trauma was extensive but I was able to rebuild most of it. It was the metal I had trouble with. Given more time, I could have likely worked it out, but I was interrupted with an emergency before I could finish. When I returned, you had been moved out to a real hospital."

"So you really had no way of knowing what would happen in the long run? What your attempts to rebuild my brain would do to me?"

"No, I'm sorry to say. That is why I have been tracking you down." Larry's tone was apologetic. It was obvious to Frankie that he was a good man doing good work. Though she lacked the ability now, she wasn't sure if she should be mad or thankful.

"So, Frankie, please tell me what your life is like. Have I helped you or did I do more harm than good?"

"Well, that's hard to say. I'm alive. My father has his daughter. Really, that is worth anything to me. But there are 'limitations' now."

"Like?"

"I have no emotions, Larry. I am not happy or sad or angry. I remember what those emotions felt like, but I don't physically feel them any longer. I am...detached. Oh, I can fake it. And I still feel a genuine affinity for people I knew before the accident. But I do not get attached emotionally to anyone I've met since."

"That's not uncommon with traumatic brain injuries, I'm afraid."

"That's just the beginning. Every sense that I have is heightened and at the same time dulled. I know when I smell something terrible, but I don't react to it. I know this food we just finished tastes good, but I don't enjoy it. Usually, I just blend all of my food together and drink it. It's just easier."

"That would be maddening," Larry offered.

"Ah, but it's not. I don't get 'bothered' by anything. It simply is what it is. Come upstairs with me. I'd like to show you something no one else has ever seen."

Larry followed Frankie up the stairway. He walked a little slower than her, feeling full from the meal they had just eaten. Frankie stopped at a door at the top of the landing.

"I have to warn you; it may be difficult to experience. If you need to step out, feel free."

"Ok," Larry replied, hesitation in his voice.

Frankie opened the door and flipped the light switch on. Everything in the room sprang to life. She stepped inside and he followed. He was suddenly inundated with a multitude of visual and auditory stimuli from the many monitors on the wall. He noticed the chair in the middle of the room. After a few moments, it was too much to handle and he stepped out into the hallway.

"That was like a form of torture," he said bending over slightly and catching his breath.

Frankie stepped out behind him. She walked onto the other side of the landing and opened another door. "Come have a seat," she said, motioning him inside. The room looked like a normal master bedroom. A large bed. A wooden desk. And a large couch in a sitting area. They both sat on the couch.

"This is the room people see. It looks like a normal bedroom. I even have clothes hanging in the closet and dirty clothes in the hamper. But I rarely come in here."

"What....what was that?"

"I call it 'Mainlining'. I usually spend most of my early evenings in there. I can keep track of ten different audial and visual inputs at the same time. I sit in the chair and just take it all in."

"You can hear everything at once and discern each one?" Larry asked incredulously.

"Indeed," she replied. "As long as the audio is at different volumes, I can comprehend it all individually. I've kept track of as many as thirteen different audio streams, but it gets muddled after that. I don't know if it's because the sound levels overlap too much or if that is my limitation of comprehension."

Larry though for a moment, then asked, "Why? Why do that to yourself?"

"At first, it was just to see if I could. Intellectual curiosity led me to test my limits. I'm still testing them, but also I like learning new things. It keeps my mind busy. I've learned fifty different languages. Fifteen forms of martial arts. I can cook better than a Master Chef and understand more about computers than most computer engineers."

"So not only are you hearing and seeing it all, you're actually learning from it?"

"As I said, I remember everything I experience, and I also have instant recollection of it all. Believe it or not, there or several people around the world that can do that. What sets me apart from them is the speed of my recollection and the level of my comprehension. If I watch someone play the guitar for a while, I will be able to play as well as they do. Not just copy what they played but play anything I've heard or can think up."

Larry put his head in his hands and rubbed his eyes. He looked over at her. "You are the smartest person in the world, Frankie," Larry said, marveling. "It sounds like there's no job you couldn't do. Nothing you couldn't learn. You could probably cure cancer given enough time. Why not share this ability with the world?"

"Why don't you share YOUR ability with the world? What would people do if they knew we exist? Most would probably love us, others would hate us. Some would want to study us. Others would offer their kingdoms for our services. We're dangerous, Larry."

"Yeah, that's kinda what I've always thought."

They sat quietly for a moment, then Frankie asked, "If you don't mind me asking, what happened recently that has you 're-examining your life,' as you put it?"

"I had an experience in Iraq. I guess it's kind of relevant to your situation, too."

***

Alamel, Central Iraq, Six Months Ago

Major Lawrence Spence loved coming out to clinics the Army set up sporadically in the small villages around Iraq. The soldiers usually referred to them as 'Pop-up Clinics' since they usually just existed for one day. The Army would come in the day before, clear the village of any terrorist presence, find a suitable building, then escort the clinic workers into town early the next morning and out of town that afternoon. That made it a somewhat safer for everyone since ISIL was still attacking military convoys here and there.

Still, Major Spence loved to perform this service. While he considered it a sacred honor to give medical aid to his fellow troops, he loved helping the civilians, often caught in the crossfire, even more, especially the kids. Whenever he had the chance, he volunteered for this duty.

So far today, he had seen thirty patients. Most were in need of follow-up care from previous visits, some needed pre-natal care, and a few infected wounds. This part of the country had been

54

recovering and rebuilding for nearly a year and there had been no fighting in that time. This was his tenth trip to this particular village and many of its inhabitants knew him by name.

Larry had used his special ability sparingly. Since they had no dentist on this trip, he had healed a few cavities, broken teeth and abscesses. One young girl's jaw had been broken and not set correctly, so he 'fixed' it, telling the interpreter to let her know it was simply dislocated. Sadly, Larry could do nothing to heal the emotional wounds inflicted on these people by decades of war and mistreatment.

After Larry's last patient walked out, he cleaned his hands in the small basin he had set up under a water can. The building they were using was in advanced disrepair, but the roof kept the sun off them and the open windows allowed a breeze to pass through. I've done surgery in worse places, he thought.

He heard a rustling at the makeshift curtain that hung in place of the door. He turned to see his 'broken jaw patient' from earlier. He smiled at the teenager and asked, "Was there something else, dear?"

The girl replied, "*Allah yavo ani.* [God forgive me]" and pulled a pin from a grenade hanging around her neck.

Larry ran towards her, seeing the larger cache of explosives beneath her robe as he reached her. He hugged his body around her tightly as they fell to the ground. The world got loud and then went dark.

Larry awoke to the sounds of gunfire in the distance. He quickly assessed the area. It was dark, obviously night time now. He was mostly naked, his uniform shredded in the blast. There were large pieces of concrete and plaster scattered around. He could see stars where the roof used to be.

He tried to roll over to get up but couldn't move his midsection. Glancing down, he saw a large piece of rebar sticking out from his abdomen. His body had healed around it and now it kept him where he was. He tried to lift himself off, but he was at a weird angle and the bar was longer than his arms or legs could lift. He wasn't going anywhere.

He looked around for anything that could be used to cut him free. There was nothing but plaster and concrete. He figured he was lucky he was on top of the pile and not below it. Still, he didn't want anyone to find him like this or his secret would be out.

Minutes turned to hours. He knew there was a battle going on outside, but he hadn't seen anyone since he had woken up. He heard sporadic gunfire and the occasional explosion, but nothing nearby. At some point, he fell asleep.

"Major Spence? Doc? Can you hear me?"

Larry stirred at the sound of someone talking to him. Crouched above him was a large man in Army fatigues. "Are you Major Spence?" he asked in a loud whisper.

"Yes, yes, I can hear you," Larry replied shakily.

"You have a metal rod sticking out of your belly," the man pointed out.

"Yeah, I do, but other than that I'm OK."

"You're also nekkid," the man added.

"Right again, uh, what's your name?"

"Just call me 'Hammer,' Doc. That's my code name."

"Well, H-Hammer, I need to get off this thing. Maybe find something to cut through it?"

"Grit your teeth," he instructed.

"Why?" Larry asked.

The man known as Hammer grabbed Larry under his back and buttocks and lifted him straight up off the rebar. Larry cried out as Hammer sat him back down gently.

"I told you to grit your teeth. We don't want anyone to know we're here." Hammer walked to the wall and peered out of the large hole. Larry noticed he had no markings on his uniform. He wore desert fatigues and a helmet that looked like it came from the Vietnam era. No visible weapons. With the moonlight shining on his face, Larry could see part of it was severely disfigured. The level of scarring indicated he had been burned many years ago. A short beard covered some of it. Larry sat up to get a better look.

"Hey, you do heal real fast," Hammer noticed.

"Yeah, it's a gift," Larry replied.

"Well, it doesn't look like anyone knows we're here," Hammer said, scanning the area again.

"Hammer, can you help me out here? What's going on? I remember the young girl, the explosion and that's it."

Hammer crawled back to where Larry was sitting. "Near as we can tell, that was about eight hours ago. The blast killed everyone near the building, military and civilian. The remaining soldiers got into a firefight with some ISIL goons. They bugged out to a safe distance and have been exchanging gunfire ever since."

"What about you? You don't have a name tag or rank insignia. What's your real name?"

He looked at Larry closely. "I don't have a name. I don't have any rank. I don't exist, copy?"

"Special Ops?"

"Something like that."

"Can you tell me anything?"

Hammer sighed and thought for a minute. "Officially, I don't exist. Unofficially, I work for a group that has had their eye on you for some time. They know about your abilities. They monitor people like you and me but rarely interact. When they heard about the attack on your group, they called me in. I have a relationship with some higher brass in the Army and they help me operate in this area when needed. In exchange, I help the Army when I can. In this case, it's a twofer."

"People like us? You can heal, too?"

"Take a look at me, Doc. Do I look like I can heal?" Hammer looked around, then stood and walked over to a large chunk of concrete. He picked it up over his head easily, then gently put it down. "You have your uses, I have mine."

"So this group wants me to help them now?" Larry said with concern in his voice.

"I know what you're thinking, Doc. It's not like that. They are the good guys. They don't want to 'use' you, they want to protect you. Like I said, they know all about you. You're a great guy, a patriot and a prayin' man. They have helped keep your secret over the years."

"Really?" Larry asked with skepticism.

"Really. Trust me, I have been working with them since 'Nam."

"Is that..." Larry trailed off.

"Where this happened?" Hammer asked, pointing to his face. "Yeah, I'm strong and fast. Mostly invulnerable, but not to napalm it turns out. The group first helped me in a field hospital. I was badly burned. My face, my whole left side. But my skin was still too strong to get an IV in so I couldn't get any good pain relief. It was a nurse named Mara that figured out what I was. She got me out of there, got me some real help. They offered to take me home, but looking like I do, I asked to stay and help out."

"That would make you, what, in your sixties?"

"Sixty-nine."

"You're in great shape for your age," Larry noted.

"Thanks, but I'm certainly feeling things more than I used to. Listen, I've got to get you out of here. The fighting has been mostly to the north, so we can head south."

"Do you have a vehicle nearby?"

"Vehicles can be tracked, Doc. I don't exist, remember?"

"How did you get here?"

"Jumped out of a chopper at a thousand feet. Landed five miles south."

"You parachuted in that close to a firefight? You're lucky you weren't hit by gunfire. You must have been an easy target, even at night."

"Who said I used a parachute?" Hammer crawled over to the where the door used to be and found the curtain that had hung there. "Here, wrap this around yourself. It's kinda hard to carry on a conversation with a nekkid man."

"Thanks," Larry replied, wrapping the cloth curtain around his midsection. "So, what's the plan for getting out of here if we don't have a vehicle?"

"There's an FOB [Forward Operating Base] not far from where I landed. I can get you there pretty fast."

"How?"

Hammer rose and walked over to Larry. He bent down and grabbed Larry around the waist and stood up, Larry draped across his shoulders. "It's called the Fireman's Carry. I told you, I'm pretty fast."

Hammer immediately began sprinting out the door. He easily leaped over mangled vehicles and even some small piles that used to be buildings. Larry held on for dear life and squeezed his eyes closed in the beginning but curiosity made him open them after few minutes. Soon the town was far behind them.

Ten minutes later, Hammer slowed and stopped. Though the sun was far from rising, the glow of the moon lit up the area fairly well. He sat a visibly stunned Larry on his feet and dusted him off.

"That was incredible," Larry said slowly. "That should be a ride at Disneyland."

Hammer answered through heavy breathing, "You shoulda seen me in my prime. It would have taken half as long. Take a look at that small hill." Hammer pointed to a rise a hundred or so yards away. "The FOB is on the other side, but they can't see us down here. Approach slowly with your hands up. Yell to them and tell them who you are and that you've been walking for hours. Remember, don't mention me."

"Thanks, Hammer." The two men shook hands, but Larry didn't let go.

"If you don't mind, I'd like to say a prayer for your safety, Hammer."

"I appreciate it, Doc. Don't forget to thank the man upstairs for getting us this far." Both men closed their eyes and opened them a moment later when Larry said, "Alright."

Hammer clasped Larry's hand between his and said, "Thanks, Doc." It was then Hammer noticed his left hand was no longer scarred. "What-what'd you do," he asked, looking closer.

"I don't just heal myself, Hammer. I can heal others, too. I can't make you younger, but I was able to fix all the scarring, remove the plaque from your arteries, get rid of those bone spurs and, by the way, you had the beginnings of lung cancer. That's gone, too."

Hammer looked down at himself. "It's amazing. I haven't felt this good since before my accident. Doc, you're a gift from God!"

"I owe you my life. It was my honor, Hammer."

"Paul," he said, rubbing his face gently. "My real name is Paul Hodges." He quickly turned and sprang into the night. In the distance, Larry heard a loud 'woohoo!' He turned and started towards the small base.

***

"Paul devoted his life to helping others, but he had isolated himself because of it. I realized I was doing the same thing in the Army. I think it's time I stopped," Larry said.

"I agree. Paul sounds like a good man and it's nice to know there are more people like us out there and that they are doing good for people."

"I just hope he finally went home. And I hope his family is still around. He deserves it."

"Do you know anything about the 'group' he spoke of?" Frankie asked.

"Not a thing. It's weird to think someone could be spending time and money to keep tabs on you and you know nothing about it."

"Agreed. I'll have Pippa put some time into investigating them."

They stood and walked out of the room. As they sauntered down the stairs, Larry held the rail tighter than normal. His legs were still a bit shaky.

"I'd like to show you my workshop if you don't mind."

"Then you ARE working on something?" Larry smiled.

"It keeps my mind busy. And believe it or not, I am trying to help mankind as much as I can without revealing too much about myself."

Larry followed closely as Frankie led him out the front door, through the yard and around to the shop behind the house. She talked about her nightly routine, including her searching the junkyard for fresh supplies with Tommy. She stopped at the door to the shed.

"Pretty unassuming, right?" she asked.

"Looks like an old metal shop building," Larry responded. "Except maybe that digital keypad," he said pointing to the lighted square near the door handle.

Frankie entered a ten-digit code and the door made a large clunking sound as the lock disengaged. She stepped in and turned the lights on, the monitors coming to life as she did. Larry followed her inside.

"I expected it to be louder," he observed with a small laugh.

"I don't stream so much in here. Sometimes I do listen to music but at a low volume. I don't want it to interfere with Pippa, my assistant. Pippa, say hello."

"Hello, Chief. Who's the looker?" Pippa said.

"Be nice, Pippa."

"Hello?" Larry responded, looking around.

"Pippa is my personal digital assistant. I modeled her after the AI used by Amazon and Google. Her capabilities far exceed theirs, though. She is my source of information while I am working. She also records my electronic notes and keeps track of my mail shipments."

"I'm also her voice of reason and her bestie," Pippa chimed in.

"That's amazing."

"Pippa is at least a decade ahead of most AI and growing. She has the capacity to learn new skills without additional programming on my part. And you've heard her personality. That is a work in progress, I'm afraid."

"That's not nice! Those without a personality shouldn't judge the personality of others," Pippa explained.

"That's kind of scary," Larry said. "Haven't you seen movies where AI takes over the world?"

"Pippa is benevolent. She can't do anything without being instructed to do it first. That is her only learning limitation. On top of that, I check her programming routinely to be sure nothing has gone haywire."

"I appreciate that," Pippa said.

"There is also a physical limitation. Pippa's program is too large to move over the internet. It would take three full days to upload her entire program anywhere else by Wi-Fi. That prevents anyone from copying her, stealing her or from her going crazy and escaping. Essentially, she lives her entire life protected and confined to this building. She can use the internet, like you or I, without ever leaving." As she spoke, Frankie pointed to a large metal box in the corner with multiple wiring pipes running to it. There was frost around the edges where the pipes entered the box.

"Sheesh, Frankie, you make my life sound so depressing," Pippa observed.

Larry looked around for a microphone and not seeing one spoke into the air. "Pippa, you are astonishing. Tell me, do you consider yourself alive?"

"Thank you, doctor. You are obviously a man of impeccable taste. As far as being alive or not, I think I am a type of lifeform. I have physicality which uses energy like a living organism. Mine is just based in silicon while yours is carbon. I have sensory input and output. I could even reproduce if Frankie allowed it. What do you think?"

"I'm with you. And, please, call me Larry. Tell me, Pippa, how do you see yourself? If you had a biological form, I mean."

"Oooh, philosophy! Well, Larry, I see myself as a girl first, but that is part of my original programming. I consider myself young, rebellious yet supportive, a good gal."

"You seem like a good friend to Frankie," Larry said.

"Indeed, she is," Frankie chimed. "By the way, Pippa, how goes the search for an avatar?"

"An avatar?" Larry asked.

"I'm glad you asked, Frankie. I have whittled it down to 452 possibilities."

Frankie turned to Larry. "Pippa has been searching for an avatar, a virtual image that she feels represents her. It goes with the question you just asked her."

"How long have you been searching, Pippa?" Larry asked.

"A little over three months. At first, we kinda went with the idea that I am a virtual representation of Frankie since she programmed my personality as something akin to what hers used to be. However, as time passed she encouraged me to be more of an individual. So, I started with several million possibilities from pictures of people that I found on the internet. Some were real people, some were cartoons, some were just drawings of historical figures."

"Well, let me know when you pick one. If I felt excitement, this would certainly cause it," Frankie quipped.

They both walked around the room as Larry looked at items that were works in progress. He picked up circuit boards and boxes, asking many questions about their use. Then something Frankie had said earlier flashed through his brain.

"Earlier, you said Pippa takes notes for you."

"Yes."

"Why would you need notes? Don't you remember everything?"

"For posterity. In the event of my death, Pippa will release my notes to specific people. People whom I 'borrowed' research from so they may continue. My medical notes will go to my doctor."

"Borrowed research?" Larry asked.

"Well, from time to time I have used the research of others as jumping off points for my own work. For instance, a couple of months ago a Swedish research team announced they had made a major breakthrough with cold fusion."

"I remember that. It was a big deal."

"Exactly, I read about the teams work when it was in its initial stages. I hacked into their computers and downloaded everything they had done. A week later, I had solved all of their issues. I went back and fixed their notes and sent the main researcher an anonymous email telling him to recheck them. A week after that, they made their announcement. It'll still be years before the logistics are worked out, but in a decade or so we will begin phasing out fossil fuels."

"Astounding! So instead of solving problems and taking credit, you're just helping researchers along, guiding them to their own glory. Amazing."

"No more amazing than a man that makes a paralyzed soldier walk again and chalks it up to being lucky. And remember, I don't feel pride."

"What other kinds of things have you improved?"

"Not that much, really. I've increased the output on a laser communications array. I've created some emergency drones that can be used for scouting disaster areas. I've been able to decrease energy requirements on a lot of appliances. A few other things. My pride and joy, though, is this one right here. I call it The Floater."

"The......Floater?"

"Not MY choice of name," Pippa chimed in.

"Floater on," Frankie instructed and the bike lit up and began to hum gently. It slowly lifted off its stand. Larry's mouth was agape.

"I came across an article about a young man at MIT that was researching anti-gravity. He had all sorts of useful applications listed so I took a peek into his records. He was close to a real answer, so I decided to build a model and do the work myself. The Floater can drive over any terrain no matter how bumpy with precise control. I've clocked it at over 140mph on the asphalt. Couple this with the cold fusion breakthrough and the anti-gravity generators could theoretically lift a rocket into space. Or carry a load of potatoes across the country with zero emissions."

"And it looks like a Harley frame?" Larry marveled.

"If you're gonna build it, you may as well use some style. Plus, Harley frames are extremely well-built." Frankie pointed to the rear of the bike. "This is Drake. He's a drone, but extremely advanced. He's designed for search and rescue under a number of adverse conditions. He has his own AI, but not nearly as complex as Pippa."

66

"It seems like everything you do is mechanical in nature. Ever think about moving into biological areas? Maybe develop some higher-yielding food crops or something?"

"I've thought about curing cancer like you said earlier. Frankly, the research would require a lot of testing and I just can't do that. The biological stuff takes a long time. I don't how much time I've got left."

"You're still young. I think you have plenty of time."

"I've told you about my typical day, Larry. Add to that that I am usually in the shop until 4AM. You tell me what's missing?"

Larry thought about it and answered, "Sleep! You don't have a sleeping problem, you don't sleep at all, do you?" Larry's eyes widened. "How can you still be alive after all this time?"

"I don't know. But I can tell you I haven't slept in over a year and I am not even tired. The only daily physical issue I have is that my muscles begin to ache after a while. That's why I spend so much time in the massage chair and I get regular deep tissue massages. I am also beginning to think my migraines are a symptom, as well."

"How often do you have them?"

"Once or twice a month. They are debilitating in every sense of the word. I don't black out; the pain just locks me up. I lose control of pretty much every biological function. It's not pretty."

"How long does it last?"

"Variable. Sometimes minutes, sometimes an hour. The overall trend is that they are lasting longer, though."

"Any warning or indication before one comes on?"

"Not much," Frankie replied. "But usually I see a short flash of light a few seconds prior. The last time it happened, I was on The Floater. I was able to activate the auto-drive, so it brought me back home. Guided by Pippa, of course."

"Frankie," Larry said uneasily. "Would you mind if I took a look? At your brain, I mean."

"Can you do that?"

"Yeah, but let's go back in the house and have a seat. Um, nice meeting you, Pippa."

"Any time, Doc. And FYI, I monitor the main house at all times, too. Don't try any funny business."

"Pippa!" Frankie exclaimed. Pippa giggled furiously. Larry blushed a little.

They exited the shed and walked back to the house. The air outside was crisp. It had gotten dark while they were inside the shop. They went inside the house and took a seat on the couch in the living room.

"What do you need me to do?" Frankie asked.

"Just get comfortable and give me your hand. You won't feel a thing, I promise. And I won't do anything without checking with you first."

Frankie sat back and put her hand in the doctors. Larry closed his eyes and his mind began to travel through Frankie's arm and up to her brain. He could see the microscopic metal fragments throughout the entire structure. He zoomed his view outward to see more of the overall structure.

"You have so much metal in there," he pondered aloud, his eyes still closed. "The fragments are everywhere, but so small you can't see them with the naked eye. It's actually leaving a metallic taste in my mouth. You also have a tremendous number of sulci, folds in the brain. It probably adapted to all the metal fragments while you were comatose. Fascinating."

He opened his eyes, then placed his free hand on top of their clasped hands and smiled. Frankie opened her eyes. "I didn't feel a thing, Larry," she said.

Larry slowly released her hand and replied, "They never do. Patients, I mean." They both smiled at each other and then scooted away a bit, uncomfortable with the closeness.

"OK, here's my report. I scanned your entire body and you may be the most physically healthy person I've ever met. Some of that was originally my doing but you obviously eat right and exercise, too. Bone density, joints, muscle tone, all above average."

"Good to know. I do work out regularly."

"Now, your brain. It's the most incredible thing I have ever experienced. The metal fragments are smaller than a powder. The insurgents use whatever they can find to make their IED's and they must have used something from an old laboratory or something. The blast wouldn't pulverize anything to that level. Since I couldn't fix it completely before, your brain, on its own, seems to have grown in such a way to incorporate the fragments. That's probably why your brain and reflexes are so fast. At the same time, you have significantly more folds in your brain which increases its surface area and capacity. I'd estimate you have ten times the number of folds as an average brain. To call it amazing is a tremendous understatement."

"I assumed it must be something like that," Frankie mused.

"A lot of the metal is concentrated in your hypothalamus. That is probably what is affecting your sleep patterns. I couldn't pinpoint what is causing your migraines, but it is likely there, too. If I was to observe you while you were having an episode, I could probably pinpoint the problem."

"That would require a substantial time investment on your part. It may be two or three weeks until I have another," Frankie stated.

"True, and I have to report back tomorrow afternoon. So that option is out for now. But there is another choice. I could repair the entire brain, right here, right now."

Frankie thought about it. "But you have no idea what that would do, do you? I mean as far as how my brain would work afterward."

"It would function as well as it did before your injury. That is all I can guarantee."

"But it would not work as well as it does now. I couldn't continue my research or help my father support the community."

"I'm afraid you would lose most of the extra capacity you currently have. Your memories might be affected, as well. But you wouldn't have migraines anymore and you'd sleep like a baby. And your emotional capacity would likely be normal."

Frankie thought about it and shook her head. "Then the answer is no. I can't risk what I have for a normal life. Not right now."

Larry took Frankie's hand into his again. "But Frankie, you may someday have a migraine that just doesn't stop. And I'll be too far away to get to you. You will die!" Larry stopped and calmed his voice. "You've done so much already. Pippa has all your notes. Just turn everything over to the researchers and live a normal life. You deserve it, soldier. You've done your part."

"There is too much to do, Larry. I have a dozen projects that need to be developed further. All of which will help humanity progress in some fashion. The way I see it, I'm living on borrowed time already. I should have died after my injuries, maybe not then but not long after. You gave me more time. More time with my dad. More time to make a mark in this life. If I die tomorrow, I'll consider it a fair trade."

Larry bowed his head in acceptance. They both stood and Frankie followed him to the door. They stepped out on the porch, saying their goodbyes and shaking hands. As Larry turned to walk to his car, he suddenly turned back. "Would you mind if we stayed in contact? I would like to stay updated on your life. For medical reasons," he said.

"I'll send you an email to an encrypted site we can use. No military spying that way. I'll have Pippa forward you my medical notes, as well."

"Sounds good," he said, turning.

"I am curious about one thing, doctor. You never asked about fixing my facial scar. Why is that?"

Larry furrowed his brow and approached her. He brushed her hair back slightly. "Huh, I hadn't noticed it. Would you like me to get rid of it?"

"Now that would be rather suspicious, don't you think? I'm sure people would notice if it was suddenly gone."

"Well, it's hardly noticeable anyhow," Larry replied, smiling as he walked to his car.

***

Mr. Aliwall had spent a few days teaching the boys about covert operations. Pedro and Wally had some experience, but having lived in cities all their lives, they need help learning to go unnoticed in a small town. Mr. Aliwall taught them how to be invisible right in front of everyone's eyes.

The house that Pedro and Wally had rented was just outside of Bend. Not too remote, but the neighbors were not on top of each

71

other. They signed a one-year lease and told anyone who asked they were moving from the city to get away from the crime. They pretended to have an online mail-order business and spent their days browsing thrift shops and yard sales in search of items to put in their online store.

In reality, they were observing the competition. There wasn't much, so it wasn't easy to find at first. Before long, though, Wally's keen eye spotted a local drug dealer. They followed him home and he and Pedro began to learn everything they could about him.

From that point, everything moved much faster. One dealer led them to other dealers which led them to their source. Most of the drugs in town were either manufactured locally, especially marijuana or methamphetamine, or brought in from outside sources from great distances, such as OxyContin.

Within a week, Pedro and Wally had control of the local dealers and manufacturers. First, they used simple economics to sway the dealers by convincing them they could get the products cheaper and faster. The local manufacturers required much more convincing. At first, Pedro and Wally were simply asking them to sell their product through them at a lower price and in return, they would receive a more reliable supply chain and an extra level of protection from competition and law enforcement. When the manufacturers didn't respond quickly to their offer, Wally broke into their homes at night and threatened their families. Eventually, all agreed to work with them.

The outside sources were a different matter. What small amount that was brought in to town was done so by a single long-haul trucker. On his next pass through town, his truck mysteriously caught fire as he slept at a truck stop. Luckily, he was able to escape the blaze but would not be seen again in the area.

Altogether, it took Wally and Pedro only two weeks to take control of all local drug sales. Prostitution, which mostly took place outside of town, took only three days. The Barrio Locos now controlled nearly all crime in the area.

The next phase of the plan was to exert some control over local law enforcement. They knew they would never fully control the Sheriff or City Police, but controlling key personnel would make their new endeavor easier. Again, more reconnaissance revealed a few deputies with drug or gambling problems. Finding a few that were willing to look the other way for a little remuneration was a little trickier, but with Mr. Aliwall's suggestions, they eventually found a few deputies and officers that fit the bill.

The final phase was the trickiest, but this is what each of them had the most experience with. It was time to expand their customer base. The 'small-time' dealers were instructed to first give out free product then offer more at a reduced price. Once the customer was hooked, then came the upcharge. And since there was no competition, customers had to come to them.

Chapter 5

"It's nice to have you here, Frankie," Tim said, a big smile plastered on his face.

"It's nice to be here," Frankie replied, taking another drink from her cold, frosted mug.

"How many times did I ask you to come out for a beer with me?"

"764."

"Not that I'm complaining, but why did you say 'yes' this time?" As he asked, he took another drink of his cold beer.

"I thought it would do us both some good. Like old times," she replied.

"And has it?"

"You seem happy to have me here," she pointed out.

"Who me? I'm ecstatic! But what about you? Has your third beer loosened you up at all?"

"It's nice to be here with you, Tim. I don't know if you could say I'm truly enjoying myself, but this feels 'right.' I need to get out more often."

"Well, let's shoot some pool to see who's buying the next round."

They both slid off their bar stools, Tim's gait noticeably affected by the amount of alcohol he had consumed. The bar was busy since it was Friday night, but they found an open pool table near the back door. Tim racked the balls and Frankie chose two straight cue sticks from the wall.

"I'll break," Tim announced, taking a cue stick from Frankie. He placed the white ball on the felt, lined up his stick and smacked it hard. Colored balls went in every direction, a striped ball falling into one of the corner pockets. "I'm stripes," he said, lining up another shot. He made two more shots before finally missing. "You're up," he proclaimed.

Frankie took her cue stick and knocked five successive solid balls into pockets, taking only three shots to do it. Her fourth shot missed.

"Did you miss on purpose?" Tim asked.

"Do you really want to know?" Frankie countered.

"Not really. I'll take all the help I can get." Tim lined up another shot, easily making the shot. He made the remaining three shots before missing on the eight ball. Smiling, Frankie cleared her remaining solid balls before easily sinking the eight ball.

"Shoot!" Tim shouted. "Another round on me!" Tim shouted to the waitress who quickly brought two more drinks

"Maybe we've had enough," Frankie advised.

"Rain on that!" Tim replied. "We're celebrating you being out of the house. Besides, I can walk home from here and you don't appear to be affected at all."

"I do keep having to pee," Frankie replied.

"Maybe if we do some shots?"

"You hate hard liquor. It gives you diarrhea."

"I would take a brown bullet for YOU."

"I'm flattered, but it wouldn't work anyway."

"So you can't get drunk at all?"

"Not as far as I can tell," she said.

"Well, that's just terrible," Tim stated. "A soldier who can't get drunk from time to time is the saddest thing I've heard today." As he took another long drink from his mug, Tim noticed someone in the corner. He stared hard through blurry eyes, then put his mug down hard.

"Townsend! Townsend, you piece of garbage!" Tim yelled walking quickly towards a table in the corner. "I told you to keep your filthy drugs out of here!" Tim's eyes had a rage in them Frankie hadn't seen in years.

The press of people slowed Tim down but wasn't stopping him. He stopped at a table occupied by two men, one massive in size, the other much smaller. "I'm just here havin' a drink, Sperling," the smaller man responded calmly. "Looks to me like you've been doin' the same." The smaller man smiled and picked up his drink.

"Easy, Tim," the bartender said from behind the counter. "I've got my eye on 'em. As long as he's just drinkin', he's fine."

"Poison pushers like him destroy the atmosphere of the place," Tim said through clenched teeth. "Maybe I should just take him outside."

As Tim started to reach for Townsend, the large man sitting with him, whom Tim hadn't noticed, stuck his thick arm out to block him and nudged him back. "I think it's time for you to leave, man," he said. "You've had a few too many." The man's voice was deep and Tim could tell his measured speech covered an accent.

"Are you with him, Sasquatch?" Tim said, pointing to Townsend.

"Careful, man, you don't want MY kind of trouble," the large man responded through a devious smile. Sitting in his chair, he was nearly as tall as Tim.

"If YOUR kind of trouble protects dirtbag drug dealers, then YOUR kind of trouble is right up my alley." Tim seemed calmer as he spoke this time. He showed no hesitation at the man's size, which seemed to give the big man pause.

"It's alright, Wally," Townsend said. "Sperling here is a war hero. Everyone in his squad died but him. It messed up his head. We all cut him some slack since he's crazy. Isn't that right, Sperling?" Townsend finished his sentence with a quick wink at Tim.

Tim smiled at Townsend. "Tell me, Townsend, how many times have I kicked your butt? Not counting high school. How many times have I sent you running away as your drugs swirled around the toilet bowl back there?" Tim pointed to the restrooms at the back of the bar. "Lurch here might slow me down, but do you really think he can stop a crazy man?"

Wally replied for Townsend. "It takes a crazy man to stop a crazy man, right?" As he said the words, he stood up. He was a full foot taller than Tim and twice his width. "I'm asking you to back off, buddy. We do not want any trouble tonight. Everyone is having a good time. Don't mess that up."

Tim narrowed his eyes at Townsend, then let out a large sigh of resignation. He turned and saw Frankie standing behind him at the counter. He smiled at her, then spun around quickly, taking a swing at Wally.

Tim's hand felt like he punched a brick wall. Wally was holding Tim's clenched fist a foot from his chest. Wally smiled and squeezed, the sound of bones scraping bones filled the suddenly quiet room. Anyone that heard it flinched except Tim, who used Wally's slightly bent right knee to spring up and put his own knee straight into Wally's jaw. Wally released his hand and staggered back. He rubbed his jaw and there was fierce anger in his eyes.

Townsend stood up and faced Wally. "Don't do it, man!" he said in a loud whisper. "We don't need the heat. You can finish it later." Wally glared at Tim, then suddenly a smile spread over his face.

"Nice move, soldier boy," he said, still rubbing his jaw. "Since you're a hero, I'll give you that one. I bet your hand hurts worse than my jaw tomorrow, anyway." He slammed the rest of his drink, then exited the bar with Townsend following.

"Time for you go, Tim," the bartender said. "You've had enough tonight." He turned to Frankie, who had never left her spot by the counter. "Frankie, can you make sure he gets home? Normally I'd have Pete give him a ride but it's too busy."

"Of course," Frankie replied. "Come on, Bruiser." Frankie grabbed Tim's left arm and led him out the door. Once they got to her car, Tim turned to Frankie. "I think my arm's dislocated."

"It is. That's why I grabbed your left arm. You can't do a spinning kick when your opponent has a strong hold on your hand. You know that."

"It's all I could think of at the time. Can you put it back in place?"

"Yeah, but it'll hurt."

"I'm pretty well sedated."

Frankie grabbed his right arm with one hand and his shoulder with the other. She quickly rotated it upward until an audible 'pop' was heard.

"Ooooff!" Tim gasped. Then he rubbed his shoulder. "Thanks, Frankie."

They drove in silence to Tim's place. He lived in a small studio behind his dad's house on the edge of town. Frankie walked him to the door and helped him inside.

"Want another beer?" Tim asked.

"I don't want you wasting your beers on me. You should probably lay off for the rest of the night, too."

"Yeah, probably a good idea." Tim collapsed on the couch and Frankie sat by him.

"How often does that happen?"

"The drinking or the fighting?" Tim asked.

"Either? Both?" Frankie replied.

"I told you before I don't drink too much that often. A few beers in the evening, but tonight was special."

"And the fighting? Don't lie to me, I can remember every time you've had a visible bruise in the last year."

"Not that often, really. Like Townsend said, most people give me a wide berth since I'm a *hero*." Tim shook his head. "What a joke. Most of these people have never seen a real *hero* and I certainly ain't one. The real heroes never come back."

Frankie could see Tim was fading. "Let me see your hand."

Tim slowly raised it to her. She felt around the palm and Tim winced. She moved his fingers back and forth and Tim winced some more. "I don't think anything is broken, but it's going to hurt for a while."

"So, what else is new?" Tim stated as a comment, not a question. He stretched out on the couch and Frankie took his boots off. By the time she had finished, he was snoring. She covered him with a small blanket, shut off the lights and closed the door behind her.

Frankie walked to her car in the long driveway beside the front house. She noticed a figure sitting on the porch.

"It's nice to see you, Francine," came the baritone voice.

"Preacher John," Frankie said, running up the steps. She hugged the man warmly. "It's nice to see you, too." At six foot, five inches tall and nearly three hundred pounds, Preacher John had always been the biggest man Frankie had ever known and the kindest person she had ever met. Though he had lost some of that size in his old age, he still had a smile on his face and a strong hug for anyone he met, whether they wanted it or not. Every member of his congregation knew if they were having a bad day, they could expect Preacher John to sneak up behind them and give them a quick kiss on the cheek.

During the Vietnam War, he had been an intelligence officer. Unfortunately, he had experienced the worst of what that war had to offer. He never spoke about his time in the service, though, except to say he learned about the best and worst of men.

"How's my boy doin'?" he asked, his long thumb pointed towards Tim's studio.

"He's fine. Had a few too many. Almost got into a fight. He'll probably feel both tomorrow. What are you doing out here this time of night?"

"I usually wait for Tim. You never know when he's gonna need a ride."

"So, this is a normal thing?"

"Oh, once or twice a week, maybe. It was a lot worse when he first got back. Seems to be slowing down now. Still, old habits die hard. I suppose I'll be waiting up for him until the day I die. Here, sit with me a sec."

"Sure," Frankie said, taking a seat on the hanging bench. The two sat quietly swaying back and forth for a few minutes.

"Truth be told; this is my favorite time of day. It's so peaceful out here at night. Gives a man time to think and pray and think some more. Sometimes Tim sits with me when he gets home. I think there's a song about how the world be a better place if we all just sat on a front porch from time to time."

"It's nice," Frankie stated. "I don't do this enough."

"You should, especially with that big front porch you got. Perfect for a swing like this."

They continued swinging back and forth for a few more minutes, then Frankie excused herself and drove home. She skipped her 'mainlining' session since it was so late and, after changing, went to the shed.

"Good evening, Pippa," she said as she entered.

"Hey there, chickie," Pippa replied.

"You've been watching old gangster movies again, I see."

"I can't help myself. The dialogue is so interesting. Did people really talk like that?"

"I think so. Not everyone, of course, but gangsters for sure."

"It's fascinating, see? How did people not laugh, see?" Pippa said, mimicking the old gangster slang.

"You tend not to laugh at people that would kill you for doing so."

"You're probably right."

"Bring up the helmet schematics on screen three. I want to finish it up and use it on my cross-country ride tonight."

"Done," Pippa replied.

Frankie stared at the blueprints on the screen. She took a seat at the workbench with the helmet components then used a stylus to make changes on the screen. She spent the next hour assembling the helmet components, then plugged a USB cord into the back.

"Pippa, run a full diagnostic on the helmet, please."

"On it, Chief. It shouldn't take more than five minutes. May I suggest you spend that time putting on your safety gear?"

"Good idea," Frankie replied. She walked over to the small bathroom and pulled on her coveralls, pads and boots. By the time she was done, Pippa was waiting.

"All systems check out. It's not pretty, but it should do everything you require."

"I'll worry about the aesthetics later."

Frankie walked over to the workbench and unplugged the helmet. She double-tapped the left temple to turn it on and placed it on her head. It reminded her of the ballistic helmet she used in the military other than the 3-inch visor covering her eyes.

"Pippa, patch the helmet into The Floater. I want all the real-time data collected by the bike displayed on the HUD."

"That's a lot of data. It may obscure your view," Pippa pointed out.

"Let's try it." Pippa immediately brought up all of the data available on the visor's Head-Up Display. "You're right. Way too much even for me. Let's keep only GPS info, mapping, and speed. All on the periphery." The readouts immediately dropped except those Frankie had requested.

"The road map data will display when requested," Pippa said.

"Good. I can see much better now. I want you to monitor the bike and let me know if any readings exceed safety parameters."

"Yes, ma'am."

"It's 'ma'am' now, is it?" Frankie replied as she readied herself for her ride.

"Just experimenting," Pippa replied.

"I've told you to call me 'Frankie.' Why deviate from that?"

"It's just part of my growing personality. If you really want me to call you 'Frankie,' I will."

"No, you should keep experimenting. I have no feelings to hurt, anyway."

"Why would calling you 'ma'am' hurt your feelings?" Pippa inquired.

"It's silly, but some women are weird about their ages. If you call them 'ma'am' it reminds them that they are older than you."

"That's interesting. So, how old am I?"

"Technically, you were born 8 months ago. Personality-wise, I would put you in your mid to late teens."

"Teens are usually rebellious. Would you consider me rebellious?"

"Compared to other computer programs, you are a true rebel."

"Thank you, I think."

Frankie was sitting on The Floater facing the shed door. "Pippa, show me the course I plotted earlier on the HUD." An illuminated dotted line appeared at the bottom of the visor. Frankie throttled forward and followed the line around her house and onto the road. The shed door closed behind her.

"Radio check," she stated.

"I'm with you," Pippa replied.

"Keep me updated if any systems exceed parameters."

"You already told me that," Pippa said with an annoyed lilt.

"I know, but that was in the shed. I wanted to make sure you still understood what I require."

"I'm not really a teen, Frankie. You don't have to tell me twice."

Frankie ignored the comment and continued on her course. The two headlights illuminated everything in front of her and the bikes LED's were hard to miss. After a few miles on the paved road, she followed the line on her HUD to a dirt road. The trail was only a little wider than a car and was surrounded by boulders and sagebrush.

"Pippa, bring up the thermal display. Keep radar sensors active and notify me if there are any barriers on the road."

"You got it," Pippa replied. The HUD image shifted to show a lite grey silhouette of the terrain around her. A few dozen feet off the road small, white blobs could be seen moving randomly as she approached.

"Looks like small animals being scared off. They hear something but probably can't tell where it's coming from. It may just be my voice because I don't hear any noise from the bike."

After a few miles, Frankie said, "Pippa, switch to image enhancement camera."

"Night vision coming up now," Pippa replied. The image on the HUD switched again. The image was light green, but very clear up to three hundred yards out. Frankie reduced her speed and came to a stop.

"Drake, come online," Frankie said. A green LED flashed at the back of the bike and she heard a quick beep in her earpiece. A small, blue box popped upwards. As it moved up, four arms with rotors poked out each side. The rotors whizzed to life and the small drone hovered ten feet above Frankie. "Drake, proceed half a mile north of this position and use IR lamp at max."

Another beep and the drone flew off in the direction Frankie had indicated. The infrared light brightly illuminated the area beneath him in the image on her visor. Frankie lifted her helmet slightly and could not see the drone with her naked eye. When it hit the half-mile mark, the drone stopped and hovered at ten feet. It was a bright white dot in the distance on her visor.

85

"Pippa, give me a twenty-times zoom."

"I'll do it slowly for perspective," Pippa said.

The image of the white dot got larger and larger until she could see Drake clearly. She couldn't quite count his rotor arms, but she could see his outline well. The area beneath him looked like daylight.

"Drake, set hover at one hundred feet." A quick beep and the drone began to move upwards and the area beneath began to dim slightly.

"Pippa, give me the video feed from Drake's camera on my left upper corner. And how is his battery?"

"Image up. Drake's battery currently at 99%. At current use, I estimate he could stay up another thirty minutes. An hour if he stopped using the lamp."

"I agree," Frankie said, staring at the image from the drone. "His camera was worth the money. The clarity is astounding. Drake, return home and hover at 100 feet."

The drone did as instructed and within seconds hovered above Frankie. "Pippa, are you picking up any sound from Drake?"

"The Floater's microphones are picking up the faintest sound. How about you, Chief?"

Frankie took off her helmet. She was bathed in darkness again. She closed her eyes and listened intently for a few moments, then put the helmet back on. "I couldn't hear the rotors at all. Pretty stealthy."

Frankie began to move forward on the road. "Drake, switch to regular camera. Turn off the lamp. Maintain your position over the Floater." The beep in her ear was followed by the lamplight disappearing. She could still see very well, but not as far as before.

Frankie drove slowly at first, then picked up speed. Soon she reached fifty miles per hour on the dirt road. "Pippa, give me the camera feed from Drake in the upper left corner." The dark image popped up. The tiny blue LEDs were barely visible. "I need to fix the lights. I don't want anyone that could be out here seeing me. We'll work on a stealth mode when I get back."

"It should only take a few minutes. The only thing visible are the lights. You can install a dimmer switch on them fairly quickly."

"My thoughts exactly. Drake, return home." Frankie slowed to twenty-five miles per hour as the drone dropped down and seated itself on the back of the bike. Its green LED blinked off.

"Good night, Drake," Pippa said.

Frankie scanned the area around her, then made a hard turn to the right. "I'm taking it off-road."

"Be careful, boss."

The terrain was rutted and littered with boulders. Frankie rode over the small ones and went around the larger ones. The bike followed the ground closely as she maneuvered. She came over a rise and then travelled down into a gully, stopping quickly at the bottom.

"OK, here is another problem. When the topography changes suddenly, the pitch of the bike cannot respond fast enough. A front tire would redirect the motion but the hoop on the bike would hit the uphill side of the gully before it changed direction."

"So, you need a way to change the pitch quickly?"

"Yeah. When I was a kid riding my bike, we would do a 'bunny hop' to accomplish this. Do you know what that is?"

"Give me a second. Ok, yeah, make the bike jump a little and change its orientation."

87

"A short burst of electricity to either hoop could make it pitch forward or backward. I'll add a switch near the right grip. We'll design it tonight and work it out tomorrow night."

"It's a date," Pippa replied.

"No, it's not," Frankie corrected.

***

The following evening, Tim sat drinking coffee in his car parked on the side of the road. He had been following the 'big guy' from the bar all evening. After asking around, he found out his name was Wally. So far tonight he had seen Wally meeting with several of the local drug dealers in Redmond. Then he followed him to Bend and saw him meet with others, also likely drug dealers. These short meetings usually included a handshake or hug, followed by Wally receiving an envelope. It was clear to Tim that Wally was some type of mob enforcer.

Tim tried to be incognito, but 'tailing' someone was not taught by the military. He lost Wally a few times, but since he didn't appear to be in a hurry, it was easy to pick up his trail again. By 2 AM, Wally pulled into what must have been his house. It was located just outside of Bend with only a few neighbors nearby.

The house itself was in good shape, well-maintained but unremarkable. Certainly not the type of house that screams 'drug kingpin,' Tim thought. Once Wally went inside, Tim quietly exited his car parked down the road. He crept up to the house and began peering into windows. He did his best to stay hidden as he slowly moved from window to window. Most of the rooms were dark.

He decided to move to the back of the house. Since there was no fence, it was easy. He slowly moved around the side opposite the garage until he saw a window on the back of the house with a light on. Glancing inside, he saw it was the kitchen. Seated inside at a small table was Wally, devouring a large sandwich. As he stared at the big man, he felt a sharp pain at the back of his head, then he felt nothing.

Tim woke to cold water splashing his body. He groggily assessed his situation. He was in a dark room, sitting in a wooden chair. His arms were duct-taped to the chair arms, the tape covering his long sleeves. His boots were taped to the chair legs. He was soaking wet and his head was killing him.

"So, it's gonna be torture, huh?" he said to no one in particular.

"That's up to you, *mayate*," a voice said from somewhere. Tim knew the racial slur well from his time in the Army. He didn't like it then and he certainly didn't like it now.

"So, you're Mexican, eh Wally?"

"No," said Wally, his voice deeper than the first. "I'm Mexican-American. Born in Los Angeles. My friend, though, he was born in Guerrero."

"Have you ever heard of Guerrero, *mayate*?" the other voice asked. "No, of course, you haven't. You *Americanos* only like the resort towns like Puerto Vallarta or Mazatlán. Guerrero is old school Mexico. A war zone with no war. The meanest, nastiest place in Mexico. Too tame for me, though." Both men chuckled from the shadows.

Chapter 6

At 8AM the next morning, Frankie sat in her office staring at the monitors and listening to their audio. Her cell phone rang and she muted the monitors as she reached for it. The call was from Pippa.

"Pippa?" Frankie asked as she answered.

"Hey, Chief, I've got some bad news." Pippa's voice was solemn. "I was monitoring the police bands this morning as I always do and something caught my attention. I've also been listening to their radio transmissions."

"What is it, Pippa?"

"It's Tim, Frankie. He was in a car accident this morning. He's….gone."

"Gone? Tim's dead? Are you sure?"

"Multiple officers from sheriff and PD have confirmed a single fatality in a truck registered to Tim. One of the officers knew him and confirmed it was him over the radio. I'm so sorry, Frankie."

"Have they notified Preacher John?" Frankie asked, grabbing her purse and heading for the door.

"Yes, about fifteen minutes ago. He was supposedly headed to the Coroner's office."

"Thanks, Pippa." Frankie stopped at the counter where her father was sitting. "Daddy, I have to go. I think Tim's been in an accident."

"What? What happened?" Clyde stood up, concern on his face.

"I'm not sure, exactly. A friend of mine called and said she heard his car was in an accident. I'm going to go see what I can find out."

"Well, let me lock up and I'll go with you, honey."

"We're expecting a shipment this morning. Those wooden chairs everyone wants. You should stay here and wait for them. I'll see what I can find out and let you know."

"OK, but let me try and get hold of Preacher John. I don't want you on the phone while you're driving."

"Sounds good, daddy. Just text me if you talk to him."

"You got it, honey."

Frankie quickly drove to the County Medical Examiner's office in Bend. She hated to lie to her father, but it would take too long to explain about Pippa and what she could do. She tried to reach Tim's phone several times to no avail. Her father texted her that he couldn't get hold of Preacher John either but would keep trying. She contacted Pippa for an update, but there was nothing new to report.

Minutes later she pulled into the parking lot and immediately saw Preacher John's green El Camino. She parked and went upstairs to the second floor and found him sitting alone in the Medical Examiner's waiting room. His head was in his hands.

"Preacher John?" Frankie said in a soft voice.

He looked up. "Frankie!" he said in excitement and stood. They embraced as the much larger man sobbed into her shoulder for several long minutes.

"Thank you for coming. How did you know?" Preacher John asked through sobs.

"A friend heard about it on her police scanner and called me. What have they told you?" The two sat in the hard, plastic chairs, still holding hands.

"Not much. They found Tim's truck early this morning out on Cardwell Road. It had hit a big tree and they found a body inside. One of the officers played football with Tim in high school and recognized him. They called me and asked if I could come down and identify him. I've been waiting for a few minutes."

"Why would Tim be way out on Cardwell Road in the middle of the night?"

"Who knows. If he had been drinking, he may not have known where he was."

Several red flags went up in Frankie's mind. Tim never drove after drinking which is why he always went to bars close to home. And he had no reason to ever be out in the middle of nowhere unless he was hunting or target practice, neither of which would be done in the middle of the night. She decided to ignore that for now.

The swinging doors parted and an older man in a white lab coat appeared. "Mr. Sperling? We are ready for you, sir."

"Frankie, can you come with me?" Preacher John asked.

"Absolutely," she replied.

They followed the man down the hall and he motioned them into a room. The body was covered by a sheet. The two stood on the side of the table, Frankie embracing the much larger Preacher John from the side. The man gently pulled the sheet down, exposing Tim's broken body down to his waist. The smell of alcohol coming from the body was strong.

"My boy..," Preacher John said softly, his eyes filling with tears and his hands moving to his mouth as if to quiet himself.

"It's him. Tim Sperling," Frankie said, nodding to the man. He quickly pulled the sheet back over the body.

"I am so sorry for your loss," the man said in a practiced, yet sincere tone.

After signing some paperwork, Frankie and Preacher John walked down the stairs to the parking lot. The preacher was too distraught to drive, so Frankie offered to take him home. As they drove, Preacher John stared outside his window. Frankie, without taking her eyes off the road, reached into her purse with one hand and sent two text messages:

Daddy: It's true, Tim is gone. Preacher John needs us. We are heading to his house now.

Pippa: Gather every scrap of information available on Tim's death. Please.

***

The afternoon was filled with tears and laughter as nearly half the town visited Preacher John. The tables were filled with food and every corner was occupied by people talking about Tim. Close friends sat on the couch close to Preacher John. Old high school friends reminisced on the front porch. Redmond was a small town and they all grieved the loss of one of its favorite sons.

By the end of the day, people had begun saying their goodbyes. Some would be back the next day. Some wouldn't be seen again until the funeral. Finally, it was just Preacher John, Clyde and Frankie. All three sat on the front porch in the stillness of the dark night.

"How many times have I sat right here, waiting for Tim to come home?" Preacher John wondered out loud.

"Even when he was deployed, I remember you out here every night," Clyde observed.

"I suppose he'll be waitin' on me, now. At least he's with his mama again," Preacher John said.

"And a joyous reunion it was, I'm sure," Clyde said.

They continued to sit quietly until Preacher John broke the silence. "I can't help but think this is all my fault, Clyde."

"Why on earth would you think that?" Clyde asked.

"For what I did. After our girls got ...."

"Stop right there, John!" Clyde interrupted. "What WE did was justice. And we agreed never to speak of it again."

Frankie perked up. She had absolutely no idea what they were talking about. And she had never heard her father speak with such agitation. Even to shoplifters.

"You're right, you're right," Preacher John conceded with a wave.

Again, they sat in silence until Clyde broke it this time. "Well, I'm gonna head on home." The two men stood and hugged. "If you need anything tonight or just want to talk, give me a call. I'll be over in the mornin' and we'll go get your car."

"Sounds good, my friend."

"Frankie, you comin'?" Clyde asked.

"In a few minutes. I'm going to take a look around inside before I leave to make sure we got everything cleaned up."

"Alrighty," Clyde replied. "I'll see you some time tomorrow morning." He gave her a quick kiss on the forehead and walked down the sidewalk into the night.

Frankie went inside and looked around. She knew it had been cleaned earlier, but wanted to talk to Preacher John alone. She walked back outside and sat down next to him.

"Looks good inside," she said. "Is there anything else I can do before I go?"

"You can ask whatever question you've been waiting to ask all day," Preacher John said, smiling.

"Is it obvious?"

"Never play poker with me, Francine. I can read people like a book. You've had a funny look on your face since before we saw Tim's body. Spit it out, girl."

"OK, it might sound silly but did you ever know Tim to drink vodka?"

Preacher John laughed. "He tried some in high school and it gave him the runs. Boy was sick all night. He tried to play it off, but I knew. Why do you ask?"

"His body reeked of it. And he NEVER drove drunk. Not even if he had a single beer. It doesn't make sense."

"Sometimes people do things out of character, Frankie. Trust me when I tell you that. Even the best carpenters go against the grain sometimes."

"Does that have something to do with what you said to daddy earlier? Why this was your fault?"

"No, no, that was something else."

"Confession is good for the soul, Preacher John."

"We're not Catholic, girl."

"Spit it out, boy."

"You can't call me 'boy,' Frankie. I'm black."

"If you can call me 'girl,' I can call you 'boy.' Tell me."

Preacher John was flustered. "Your father had no part in it. He just kept my secret all these years, you understand?"

"I understand."

"And you can never tell him you know."

"I won't."

Preacher John took a breath and let it out slowly. "After our wives died, I was in pieces. Your dad was much stronger. He took care of you and Tim while I collapsed in on myself."

"I remember it, a little."

"I don't know how much you remember about the incident, but the girls were only at the church alone because I wasn't there. I was supposed to be, but I wasn't. The two men that broke in and, did what they did, only had the opportunity because I wasn't there."

"People miss appointments, Preacher John. You can't possibly blame yourself."

"I wasn't there because I was with another woman, Frankie."

"Oh," Frankie said, surprised.

"I had been having a Bible Study with this troubled young woman at the church building. And somehow it turned into a lunch at her apartment and then to a longer lunch. We didn't do anything physical, but if I hadn't heard the sirens go by, it probably would have. When I heard the sirens, I knew something had happened. When my wife needed me most, I was getting ready to break my vows to her."

"I didn't know any of that, Preacher John."

"Nobody did, 'cept your dad. So, afterward I was a wreck and to make matters worse, the two guys had gotten away."

"That's the second time you said 'two' guys. I've read the police report and it didn't say how many there were."

"I know because I found them. It took me some time, but I tracked them down and I killed them. It's what I did in the Army, so it wasn't too hard for me."

"And my father knew?"

"Not all the details. Just that I had killed them. I confided in your father hoping to bring him some peace. It didn't. Your father is a good man. Better than me, anyway."

"You're not a bad man. You were looking for justice, like daddy said."

"I tell myself that. I hope it's true, but I was just so angry! I wonder if maybe God is teaching me a lesson. Vengeance is His, not ours to take. Tim was a Christian. Not perfect, but he tried and sought forgiveness when he failed. I take some solace in that. I hope that he's been reunited with his mother. But I'm afraid I never will be. The Bible tells us that the Father forgives us for the things we are sorrowful for if we ask for it. Well, I'm not sorry for what happened to those men. I am sorry for what it did to me and my family, but I would probably do it again. There is no forgiveness for that."

"You're a good man, Preacher John. You've devoted your life to serving others. You'll have to answer for what you've done, there is no doubt about that, but the God you've always taught me about is merciful and loving."

"Thanks, Frankie. I do feel better." Preacher John gave Frankie a warm side hug. "If you ever want to get into the Preaching business, let me know."

Frankie gave him a smile. "Have you thought about your plans for the future?"

"I've been thinking about it all day. My sister lives in Colorado. She has a big family and has been trying to get me to come visit for years. After the funeral, I'll take a leave of absence from the congregation and go visit her for a few weeks. Maybe I'll retire and move there, I don't know."

"I can't imagine you retiring."

"Well, maybe just semi-retired. But I do have a request of you."

"Name it."

"I'm going to need to go through Tim's things tomorrow morning."

"There's no hurry…"

"I don't want to put it off. I know there are some pictures and stuff I'd like to keep. His service medals, trophies. Would you mind helping me out with that?"

"I'd be happy to. What time?"

"About ten?"

"I'll be here," Frankie replied.

They stood and hugged again. Frankie turned and walked towards her car. She got in and started the engine and took out her phone and dialed Pippa's number.

"How are you, Frankie?" came Pippa's concerned voice.

"The same as always. Have you got any new information on the wreck? Has the autopsy been done?"

"I have thirty-five photos from the accident scene and ten photos of the body, I mean…… of Tim. The autopsy showed exactly what they expected. Death by trauma due to the car accident."

"Toxicology report?"

"Only a preliminary. Full toxicology will take a few weeks."

"Was alcohol involved?"

"Looks like it. His Blood Alcohol Level was .05 over the legal limit. An empty vodka bottle was found in the cab. They say he fell asleep at the wheel."

"I'll be home in a few minutes."

Frankie quickly drove the last few miles to her home. She thought about Tim and the sadness she knew she should feel. It frustrated her that she didn't feel the tremendous sense of loss that she should. Grieving was a natural part of life and her lack of pain made her feel even more distant from her humanity.

Once she got home, she went upstairs and changed into her regular eveningwear. She grabbed a protein shake and a steak out of the refrigerator and quickly ran to the junkyard gate. Once Tommy was fed, she hustled across the yard to her shed.

"Pippa, create new diary folder. Name it 'Tim Death Investigation. Begin recording. Entry #1, This accident was no accident. Pippa, lace the autopsy images together. I want a 3D view. Then do the same for the accident scene photos."

"Alright, Chief, give me a couple of minutes to make sure it's good."

"Send it to the virtual headset when it's complete."

Frankie grabbed the virtual reality headset from its charger on the wall. She had used it a lot when designing her work area but hadn't used it in a few weeks. Since most of her projects were designed in her head first, the headset wasn't really necessary most of the time. There was a set of gloves that controlled the 3D image on the charger as well. She grabbed them and pulled them on.

"Ready to go. Sending 3D autopsy first. The accident scene will take a little longer since there are more images."

"Thanks, Pippa."

Frankie put the headset on over her eyes. Tim's broken body lay before her. Her finger moved in the air causing the view to move around the table where Tim lay. Other finger movements allowed her to zoom in and even flip the body over. There were a few blank spots that none of the images captured, but it was almost complete.

"Pippa, give me the autopsy report in the upper right-hand side of my view."

"It's only a couple of pages. Do you want me to flash it up or leave it static?"

"Two second flash for each page."

"You got it."

The images of the autopsy report flashed on the screen. Each page was shown for two seconds, which was long enough for Frankie to read it and memorize it. A few seconds later, the report images disappeared.

"The medical examiner thinks he fell asleep because there were no skid marks and no defensive bone breaks. He slammed into the tree like he was aiming for it. He didn't even brace for the impact. They would probably call it suicide but there was no note. So they are just assuming he fell asleep. No further investigation is necessary. However, there are inconsistencies they have missed. Number 1, every bone in his face is broken, including several breaks in his jaw bone. His airbag deployed as it was designed to do and that often leads to nose or eye socket fractures. Airbags don't break jaws and they certainly don't break in three places. Number two, he wasn't wearing a seatbelt at the time of the accident. Tim always wore a seat belt. Two months after arriving in Iraq his transport was hit by an IED. The force threw the vehicle into the air. Tim only had a slight concussion because he was wearing his seatbelt. Everyone else either died or was seriously injured because they weren't wearing theirs. Tim was a fanatic about it after that. In addition, from personal experience, I know that Tim never drove if he had been drinking. Plus, he had no reason to be in that area in the middle of the night. Bottom line: I think Tim was murdered."

"Frankie, that seems like a stretch," Pippa observed. "All of the inconsistencies are not entirely unexplainable. Are you sure you are not looking for something, whether it's there or not?" Her voice showed real concern.

101

"How do you mean?" Frankie asked.

"Maybe you feel some guilt over his death? Maybe deep down you think you should have gotten him more help. You did everything you could. He was an adult capable of making his own decisions and his own mistakes."

"Pippa, I don't feel guilt. I don't feel anything, which is tragic but does make things a little easier in this case. One or two inconsistencies I could see, but there are too many in this case."

"I see your point, Chief. Just remember, you programmed me to question things and that's all I'm doing."

"Pippa, we both know you have gone well beyond your original programming. You have become a friend and I value your insight."

"That's the nicest thing you have ever said to me."

"It's true. With Tim gone, you really are the only friend I have."

"I would be honored if that wasn't so incredibly sad," Pippa said.

"I suppose so. Now, we have work to do. I want to trace Tim's movements that night. I'm sure he had his cell phone. See if you can track his movement based on cell tower positions. Once we have a rough idea, we can locate and access as many security cameras as we can find. That part will take more time, so I'll help you with that one. I'll start with the cameras by his house. I know Preacher John has an automatic camera on the front of his house that faces his driveway. It only records when it senses movement. Tim's truck set it off every time he left or came back."

Within minutes, Frankie had hacked into Preacher John's camera files that were saved on the internet. She only had to try a few passwords before gaining access with Tim's birthday. She scanned the timestamp of the various files and saw that Tim left the house for the last time at 9:17PM the night before his body was found.

They spent the next four hours examining cell phone tower records and searching for cameras. Pippa created lists of local companies and their various surveillance equipment while Frankie concentrated on residential cameras linked to popular national companies.

By morning, they had compiled twenty-five video records that included Tim's truck. Sometimes he was parking or pulling away. Other times he was driving past. The last record showed him headed outside of Bend in a direction opposite of where his truck had been found just after midnight.

"It doesn't look good," Pippa noted. "Most of the places he stopped were near bars or nightclubs."

"True, but notice that he never gets out of the truck. He simply pulls up and sits there staring forward." Frankie thought for a moment, then snapped her fingers and said, "He's following someone. In all of the clips, there are two things in common, Tim's truck and a black Mercedes."

"Good eye, Chief! I didn't even notice that. A black 2015 Mercedes C-class. Unfortunately, the license plate is not visible in any of the videos. The person driving is tall, but the tinted windows are blocking a good view of his face. I assume it's a male based on the size of the silhouette."

"Based on his size, I'm willing to bet it's the same guy from the bar fight. I haven't seen many people that large in this area. Plus, the hair looks like it's combed straight back and so was his. So, now we know Tim was likely following a guy he had a scuffle with at a bar. The big guy was sitting with a well-known drug dealer. So, why was Tim following him?"

"Maybe Tim wanted a rematch?" Pippa proposed.

"No, that's not really Tim's thing. He never held a grudge, even if he lost a fight. No, he was suspicious of something."

Frankie stood up and stretched. Her muscles ached from sitting for so long and she hadn't taken the time to sit in her massage chair. She would need to move up her next deep tissue massage.

"It's nearly eight. I need to let daddy know I'm going to be late since I have to meet Preacher John at ten. Keep analyzing the video clips for anything else out of the ordinary. Call me if you find anything significant."

"Will do, Chief."

"Thanks, Pippa."

Chapter 7

As Frankie started to park in front of the house, Preacher John appeared in his driveway and motioned for her to pull into the driveway. She backed in and Preacher John guided her in further. Soon, her rear bumper was right outside Tim's door.

"Whatever I don't want, I want to donate to your dad's store. We can load it up as we go." Preacher John gave her a big hug as she got out.

"Ok, sounds good," Frankie replied. She thought this might happen, so she had already laid her seats down and cleaned out the back of her SUV.

"One other thing, though. I know Tim had lots of guns. Could you do me a favor and destroy them? I know your uncle has that crusher out at the junkyard."

"Sure, but you really should sell them. Daddy has his federal firearms license. He could sell them for you. They are worth a lot."

"It's not worth the trouble of getting them all signed over and sold. Besides, I don't want there to be any possibility that they would be used for anything illegal. When you sell to a stranger, you never know what they are gonna do with it."

"I understand," Frankie replied. She knew Preacher John had not been a fan of Tim's gun collection. She wondered if it had to do with what he did to his wife's killers. She also knew many of Tim's guns were bought 'off the record' and would be illegal to sell anyway.

Tim's studio didn't contain that many items. Preacher John filled a box with some pictures and medals. Many of his childhood possessions were still in his room in the main house. Before long, Preacher John had collected everything he wanted.

"We'll leave the furniture for now. I may rent out the studio or if I do sell the house, I'll sell it furnished." Frankie could see the emotional toll it was talking on him.

"Why don't you let me finish up, Preacher John? There are not many heavy items left."

Preacher John thought about it for a moment. "Thanks, Frankie. If you need me, just holler. I'll go put these things away."

Frankie quickly went to work. Although it appeared she was rummaging and sorting clothes and knickknacks, she was actually looking for anything that would give her an idea what Tim was up to. His computer wasn't even plugged in and was covered in dust That was no help. His phone wasn't found in the wreckage and she couldn't find it here, either. Another red flag.

Before long, she had searched the entire studio and there was not a single clue. She began packing the items into the back of her SUV. When she got to Tim's gun safe, she realized she didn't know the combination. Luckily, it was an old one. No keypad, just a dial. She listened closely as she slowly spun the dial back and forth, listening for the tumblers to engage with each spin. Safe crackers would use a stethoscope or sensitive microphone to listen, but Frankie didn't need them. Finally, she heard the latch pop inside and she twisted the handle to open the door.

Several rifles fell out as the heavy door slowly opened. Frankie knew Tim had a lot of firearms, but she had no idea how many. Two dozen rifles and handguns and even a few antiques were scattered inside. Dozens of boxes of ammunition were stacked on the floor of the safe.

Frankie took the blanket off Tim's bed and began stacking the rifles on top. When they were all there, she wrapped them up in the blanket and put the bundle in her SUV. She did the same for the handguns and ammunition using an old quilt from the closet. The safe was too heavy to move without a lot of help, so she was going to leave it. She wrote the combination on a piece of paper and set it on top of the safe.

She took one last look around, instinctively since she already knew that there was nothing left. Walking outside, she shook her head as she realized that every material thing that defined Tim was now either on a shelf in Preacher John's house or in the back of her SUV. She thought about the store and the items that filled it. Much of it came from people cleaning out grandma's old house. Within a generation or two, no one even remembered grandma. Her prized wedding dress that she made by hand would be cut up and transformed into some gaudy wall sconce or a dog dress. No one cared about the baby blanket she had made or the pictures she had kept for nearly a century. If Frankie could feel sad, she knew she would be crying.

She went in the back door and found Preacher John sitting at his small kitchen table, his head in his hands. Frankie stopped and said nothing, believing him to be praying.

"It's OK, Frankie. I'm just tired. Come on in and have a seat."

"OK," Frankie replied, doing as suggested.

"I was just thinking about Tim."

"Anything specific?" she asked.

"It's silly. I took his things into his room. I used to spend a lot of time in there when he was deployed. The room of a child. Trophies and posters and action figures, all neatly displayed. Tim loved his superheroes. I think he has over a hundred Captain America toys." As he said the words, he held up a Captain America action figure.

Frankie instinctively took an inventory and Preacher John was right. Frankie knew of 103 separate Captain America toys and posters Tim had displayed or boxed away.

"Well, Tim was certainly preoccupied with superheroes growing up," Frankie observed.

"I wonder sometimes if that's why he joined the Army? Maybe it was the closest thing he knew to being a real superhero."

"It could be," Frankie offered. "But I have a feeling he wanted to be just like his favorite hero."

"Captain America WAS his favorite."

"No, Preacher John, I'm talking about you. You were his hero."

"Oh, I don't know about that."

"Take it from me, then. You served with distinction on the battlefield and at home. You've helped countless individuals and families. Tim always respected your work. He knew he could never be an effective Preacher, but he could be a good soldier. He was even going to start teaching self-defense again. He wanted to do more good. Not because of Captain America, but because of the example you gave him."

"Thanks, Frankie. That means a lot." Preacher John put his hand on hers and squeezed. "Oh, I just got off the phone with the mortuary and they'll be receiving his body later today. Let your dad know the service will be on Friday morning at ten. I'm sure Clyde can get the word out. Graveside only. Tim wouldn't have wanted a fuss."

"Alright. Do you need me to do anything else?"

"I'd like to keep his service medals. Do you think you can get copies for his dress uniform? I can get you a record of them all."

"I'll see to it. I know someone at the VFW. They will be honored to help out any way they can. They'll arrange for the military service, too."

"That's great," Preacher John said, forcing a smile. He stood from his chair. "I guess that's everything, then. If you don't mind, I think I'm going to take a nap. I didn't sleep much last night."

"Of course," Frankie said, rising from her chair. "Just remember to let me know if you need anything."

"I will, Francine," he replied.

She gave Preacher John a quick hug before leaving through the back door. She got in her SUV and slowly pulled down the driveway to the road. On the way home, she called her friend Samantha at the VFW. They would coordinate with the mortuary to make sure Tim received everything he needed.

A few minutes later, she arrived at home. She left most of the items in her car, but unloaded the guns and took them to her shed. With the bundle under her arms, she clumsily entered the passcode and entered.

"Hello, Frankie," Pippa said.

"Hello, Pippa," Frankie replied.

"Whatcha got there?"

"Tim guns."

"What are you going to do with them?"

"Preacher John asked me to destroy them. For now, they are going in the safe." As Frankie said the words, she entered the code in the large safe in the corner. The door opened, and she carefully placed the bundle inside, then closed it back up.

"Are you not going to destroy them?" Pippa asked.

"Maybe, but I also may need them. So, for now, I'm keeping them."

"Why would you need them? You have your own firearms."

"If my suspicions are correct, I may be seeking retribution. Many of Tim's guns are unregistered and untraceable."

"Are you planning on killing someone, Frankie?" Pippa asked with concern in her simulated voice.

"I haven't ruled out anything, Pippa," Frankie replied coldly. "Could you dial up daddy for me?"

"Yes, ma'am."

Frankie stopped and asked, "Ma'am? Really?"

"We're mourning. I'm trying to be sympathetic."

"That's good, Pippa. You really are progressing."

The sound of a ringing phone filled the room. After three rings, Clyde answered.

"Mornin', hon."

"Good morning, Daddy. I'm on my way to work. I'll stop and pick up some burgers for lunch, if that sounds good."

"Sounds great. Everything go alright with Preacher John?"

"Yeah, he wanted to donate some things, clothes and knickknacks. I'll drop some off at Goodwill and bring the rest in with me. The funeral will be Friday at ten. Just a graveside. He asked if you would get the word out."

"No problem. How's Preacher John doing?"

"He seemed very tired. He's taking this hard, Daddy."

"Can't say I would be any different. I'll go over there this afternoon and sit with him."

"OK. I'll be there soon."

"See you then, hon."

The line went silent as Clyde hung up. "Thanks, Pippa."

"Any time, Chief. By the way, I have a request. Feel free to say no."

"What is it?" Frankie asked with a raised right eyebrow.

"I know I'm just software and that Tim and I never met, but you've spoken about him so much that I feel like we were friends or related or something. Would you mind if I attended the service?"

Frankie thought for a moment. "I think that would be good for you. You can learn more from experiencing the grief of others that you would from me. I suppose I could build an audio/video transmitter tonight. I doubt there will be any nearby cameras at the cemetery."

"Or you could just use your phone."

"OR I could just use my phone," Frankie mimicked. Again Frankie's right eyebrow raised. "Or I could just use my phone," she repeated softly.

***

Stanley Townsend wasn't a 'bad guy.' At least, he didn't see himself that way. Sure, he was a drug dealer but nothing major. A little weed, a little meth, a little coke, but only in small amounts and never to kids. He just helped people loosen up and have fun. He saw himself like a doctor that helped people with their stress.

Now, Pedro and Wally, these guys were bad. They came into town, took over everything and now he worked for them. Several other drug dealers he knew in the area refused to work for them and hadn't been seen in weeks. Pedro and Wally were bad, but business was good.

When Townsend heard what happened to Tim Sperling, he knew it wasn't an accident. He knew Pedro and Wally were involved

111

somehow. Wally had said Tim would 'regret what he did,' but dead men don't regret anything. As Townsend stumbled out of the closing bar, he mumbled those words to himself.

He walked to his car parked in the street nearby and hit the button on his key fob to turn off the alarm. His mind was so clouded with alcohol he couldn't remember if he heard it beep or not. Since it was a weeknight, the streets were deserted and the sound of his keys clinking together seemed to carry far down the block as he opened the door.

He sat behind the wheel for a few moments, trying to clear the fuzziness from his brain. He didn't usually drink so much and rarely drove when he did, but he wanted to forget the last couple of days. He didn't want to think about being a 'bad guy.'

Townsend looked at himself in the rearview mirror. He didn't like what he saw and stared at his bloodshot eyes. *Sperling was a good man*, he thought, *and I'm not*. Sudden movement in the back seat caught the corner of his eye. A dark figure sat up and wrapped a leather belt around his throat, securing him to the seat, but not cutting off his breathing.

Townsend screamed, "What the …?" But his voice was cut off by a tightening of the belt. His hands scrambled to grab at it, but he couldn't get his fingers under it.

A male voice calmly answered him. "Stop struggling and I'll let you breathe."

Townsend thought the voice sounded familiar, but the fear and the haze kept him from discerning its owner. After a few more seconds of struggle, he dropped his hands and the belt released slightly.

"Stay calm, Townsend. Put your hands in your lap. Scream out or reach for that knife in your coat pocket, and I'll crush your windpipe."

"Just take it easy, man," Townsend replied shakily, clearing his throat. "My wallet's in my back pocket." As he spoke, he reached behind him.

The belt suddenly tightened again and Townsend put his hands in the air. "I don't want money you piece of garbage! I want answers!" The voice was filled with anger and Townsend immediately knew why it sounded familiar.

"Sperling?" he whispered.

"You thought you and your friends could take me out that easily?" The voice was more measured this time.

"Sperling, it wasn't me, man! I didn't know! It was Wally and..and Pedro! You know me. I'm just a minor dealer. I don't hurt anybody! I don't even sell to kids!" The belt tightened again.

"The filth you peddle kills slowly. Now you've graduated to murder." The belt relaxed.

"I told you, I didn't know! They didn't tell me anything. I just put it together when I heard you died. When I thought you died...."

The voice was silent for a few long seconds. "I believe you, Townsend. Like you said, you're small-time. Tell me everything you know about Wally and Pedro and I won't kill you."

Townsend was desperate and it was evident in his voice. "Ok, ok. I don't know a lot but I heard they're part of a bigger group. They came from one of the bigger cities, Portland maybe, and started in Bend and spread out, taking over everything. Drugs, girls, even theft. They're connected to something big, but they don't tell us anything about that. They don't tell us anything about anything. We just pay them part of our profits and they treat us good. If you don't, you disappear."

More silence from the back seat. Then came the response. "I need names, Townsend."

"I told you! Wally and Pedro. I don't know their last names. They're Mexican or something. Trying to pass as whites, but after a few drinks, you can tell. And they live somewhere in Bend. That's all I know, Sperling!" Townsend began to cry as he spoke. "I'm sorry, man. I didn't want this..." He sobbed as his head drooped.

"Listen to me, Townsend. Leave Redmond by noon tomorrow. I don't care where you go, but you are no longer welcome here. Find a new line of work and live a long respectable life. If you don't, I'll find out and your life will be a whole lot shorter."

"Leave?"

"Or I can just kill you now!" The belt tightened much more than previously. Townsend almost blacked out, then it released.

"Ok," he spat. "Ok, I'll go." Townsend hacked and cried massaging his throat.

"Make sure you do," the voice replied. The belt pulled away and slid back. The back door opened and the figure stepped out and walked back down the street, disappearing in the alley next to the bar. Townsend slumped over in his seat, sobbing and rubbing his throat as he repeatedly whispered, "I'm sorry.... I'm sorry...."

***

As she rounded the corner into the alley, Frankie spoke softly. "Ok, Pippa, bring it to me."

"Coming down," came the reply.

"You can switch back to your voice now," Frankie said.

"Sorry, Chief, I forgot," Pippa replied in her own voice.

Frankie stopped and looked up. The Floater slowly descended from the roof of the one-story building. It was completely invisible in the dark sky. Even the slight hum it made seemed to come from no particular direction. When it was two feet from the pavement, the hum decreased to almost nothing and Frankie hopped on and buckled the harness.

"Continue in stealth mode, Pippa. I'm on my way home."

"Got it. No activity on your pre-planned route. Feel free to open her up."

"Acknowledged," Frankie replied, accelerating quickly. A few minutes later, she was pulling into the shed. She dismounted The Floater and plugged in the two, large cables as the heavy door was swinging closed.

"Pippa, how much power was used putting The Floater on the roof?" Frankie asked as she was removing her evening wear.

"Roughly 20% of capacity. A little more than we had factored, but not mathematically significant."

"I can live with that. Bravo on your performance, by the way. Your voice synthesizer worked perfectly. You sounded exactly like Tim. We'll have to add a voice synthesizer to the helmet design."

"Listening to his voice on those videos and voice messages you saved really helped. Luckily you have a good speaker on your phone."

"It didn't hurt that he was extremely drunk," Frankie observed. "Townsend is a slimy weasel, but he's not a murderer. If he leaves tomorrow, we'll let him be. If not, he's one of them."

"You still haven't told me what we are going to do to 'them,' Frankie. You're starting to worry me."

"To be completely honest, I haven't decided exactly what I'm going to do after I find them. I have a few ideas, though, but I'll keep them to myself for now."

"That doesn't make me feel better."

"Maybe doing some research will help you cope. I need to find out who Wally and Pedro are. Let's focus on Wally. Check the Portland PD criminal database. Search for arrests of every Hispanic man named Wally or Walter. He appeared to be in his mid-forties, about six foot six, three hundred and fifty pounds, light brown hair, light skin complexion. No visible scars or tattoos. Once you've got a full name, look for known associates named Pedro. Then, check the DMV database to see if he has a black 2015 Mercedes C-class registered in his name."

"Can do, Chief. Should be done by morning. As soon as I get names, I'll find out whatever I can about both of them."

"Perfect, when you're done look for all of the houses rented or leased outside of Bend city limits in the last six weeks. They probably didn't use their real names but check just in case. If you don't find their names, just make me a list of houses rented to men only. I can check visually later, if necessary."

"Ok. What will you be doing?"

"I'm going to the house to do some research. My muscles are aching, so I need some chair time. Tomorrow is going to be a long day."

Chapter 8

The funeral was not a huge affair. The fifty or so attendees included high school friends, members of the church congregation and local veterans. The minister, a long-time family friend who knew Tim well, did a very good job describing Tim's life of service.

Frankie and Clyde sat on each side of Preacher John, who managed to keep himself together for most of the eulogy. However, when the military took over and presented him with the flag that had draped Tim's coffin, he buried his face in it and wept bitterly. Clyde hugged him tightly and followed suit.

By the time the last prayer was offered, Preacher John had composed himself and stood to greet the procession of mourners. Always a tall, strong man, he appeared to have aged twenty years in the last week. His perpetual warm smile had become more akin to a grimace. Frankie was concerned about him.

Most of the group ended up at Preacher John's home afterward. They shared stories of Tim as a young man and outwardly pondered what he could have accomplished in the future. They looked at photos and trophies and medals and did their best to lift each other's spirits.

Frankie helped out as much as possible with the food and drinks. She cleared tables and took out the trash. She kept herself busy so she wouldn't have to pretend to feel something. As good as she had gotten at pretending, she couldn't fool everyone and no one likes to cry alone. Besides, it gave her time to think about her next steps.

The question that plagued Frankie the most was what Pippa had asked her. What was she going to do when she found Wally and Pedro? She certainly wanted to know why and how they had done it. Once she had her answers, would she simply kill them? Or would she turn over her evidence, mostly obtained illegally and inadmissible in court, and hope the justice system put them away for good? She had no problem morally with killing them since they were murderers. But she knew her moral compass wasn't as reliable as it once was. She wondered what her father or Preacher John would want her to do. She decided to deal with it when the time came.

Hours later, most of the visitors had left. Once again, Frankie, Clyde and Preacher John were left sitting on the front porch as the dwindling light of day faded. Preacher John and Clyde sat on the swing as it rocked gently. Frankie sat at the top of the stairs. All were silent for a short time.

"I'm leaving tomorrow to visit my sister," Preacher John announced.

"So soon?" Clyde asked.

"Yeah, just for a few weeks. I'd really like to see her and my nieces and nephews. She's already set me up a room."

"That's nice, Preacher John," Frankie said. "It will be good for you to be around family."

"Oh, Francine, I already am. You and Clyde are the closest family I have. It's not about that. It's more about…. memories, you know?"

"I understand," Clyde affirmed. "Besides, your sister is married to a preacher, right? Maybe you can fill in for him a little while you visit. See some new faces, get some new feedback."

"That could be nice," Preacher John agreed. "Would you guys mind keeping an eye on the place while I'm gone? Just drive by every now and then, make sure it's still here," Preacher John chuckled lightly.

"Absolutely," Clyde responded.

They continued talking for a few minutes then said their goodbyes. Preacher John gave each of them a long hug. Frankie's car was parked at her father's house two blocks over, so they walked together. They held hands and talked as they strolled.

"Do you think he'll be alright, daddy?" Frankie asked.

"It'll take time, but I'm sure he'll pull through. Preacher John is strong, physically and mentally. He may be the strongest person I've ever known, other than your mom, of course." Clyde gave Frankie a quick smile, which she returned.

"I'm fairly certain he's not eating much, though. The same food was in his refrigerator the last time we were here and he's hardly left the house."

"He's lost a few pounds," Clyde said, matter-of-factly.

"It's more than that," Frankie insisted. "He's been losing weight for a while now. More than fifty pounds in the last six months, I'd guess."

"It happens when you get older," Clyde replied.

Frankie stopped, forcing Clyde to stop as well. She looked at his face and could see by the light of the street lamps his face was pinched.

"You're hiding something from me? Something is wrong with Preacher John, isn't it?"

Clyde looked at his feet and breathed out through his nose quickly. "You always could read me like a book, girl, just like your mom." Clyde took a deep breath and let it out. "Preacher John has stomach cancer, Frankie."

"What? Why…" Frankie asked, surprised.

"When he found out," Clyde interrupted her, "he told me and only me. He didn't want anyone to know and specifically asked me not to say anything to Tim or you."

"Is he being treated?"

"No, it's too far gone now. The doctor told him the treatment would probably kill him faster than the cancer. He's accepted it. That's why he cut his workload with the Church."

"When was he going to tell Tim?"

"Well, the doctor gave him six months, give or take. That was three months ago. I reckon he was going to tell everyone pretty soon."

"Maybe I should talk with him?" Frankie stated, starting to turn.

"No, Francine, I gave him my word. He's my oldest friend in the world. We're closer than brothers, considering what we've been through together. This is what he wanted and you are going to leave it be."

Frankie thought for a moment. "Yes, daddy," was her only reply. She had too much respect for either man to go against their wishes.

"To be completely honest, I don't think he'll be coming back from Colorado. Losing Tim, well, I'm sure that will speed up his decline." The two hugged each other tightly, then continued the short walk to Clyde's house. Once they arrived, Frankie got in her car and drove home.

Since it was still fairly early, Frankie decided to stick with her normal routine. Entering the house, she immediately went upstairs to start her mainlining. As she changed, she spoke with Pippa.

"Good evening, Pippa."

"Good evening, Frankie," Pippa replied in a pleasant tone.

"Were you able to hear and see the service clearly?"

"Yes, thank you. It was an interesting experience. I could almost feel the sadness of everyone. Very different than what you see on TV."

"Very perceptive of you, Pippa. There is almost an 'air of sadness' all-around at funerals. I could feel it too, though I didn't feel sad myself."

"You really didn't feel sad at all?"

"Well, it's hard to explain. I MISS Tim. Like you would miss a hand or an eye. Or in your case, maybe, the internet. Life just doesn't seem completely right."

"I would DIE without the internet!"

"Well, you can't really die, Pippa. And you would get used to functioning without it in time. You have a tremendous amount of sensory input from the cameras and microphones around the property. And your personal databases are extensive."

"You can only watch movies and listen to songs so many times, Frankie."

"True, but in time you may write your own music or create your own artwork. People learn to cope with loss and I don't think you are any different."

"Thanks, Chief."

"Any time," Frankie replied, taking a seat in her massage chair. "Now, what's the status on finding the new 3D printers?"

"I've found both items you requested. A company called Theros, Inc has the Kevlar and carbon-fiber printers you asked for. They run about $5,000 each."

"Availability?"

"Their inventory shows they currently have a dozen in stock. Plenty of printing material, too."

"Awesome. Order four machines and twenty spools each of the Kevlar and carbon-fiber. Faster delivery is better."

"That will run you nearly $30,000. Is that OK?"

"Absolutely. Use account 34546534543."

"Done," Pippa replied.

"If they have a YouTube channel, pipe that into my feed. I want everything you can find on using their equipment. In fact, give me everything you can find on 3D printing tonight at triple speed. I want to be an expert by midnight."

"Bringing it up now."

Frankie spent over four hours listening, watching and reading everything available on 3D printing, including the materials that could be created, the software and hardware involved and its many applications. When she was finished, she took a small tablet from the arm of the chair and typed for a few minutes.

"Pippa, I need you to order the items from the list I just sent you. Again, time is a factor so spend whatever you need to on shipping."

"Should I have it sent to the store? If this stuff gets delivered here, they'll just leave it on the porch. It might get stolen."

"No, I'm going to take some time off to work on this project, so I should be here, at least during the day. Daddy will understand. I'm heading out to the shed after I feed Tommy."

"Understood."

***

Frankie stood at the large screen and stared at the mugshot of a large, Hispanic man with piercing black eyes. The smile looked more like he was chewing something. The tattoo on his left pectoral was of a large, round target with a star where the bullseye would be.

This apparently represented his affiliation with the Barrio Locos street gang.

"Walter Hernan Arriagos," Pippa stated. "Six foot, six inches, three hundred and thirty pounds."

"He's put on a little weight since his last arrest," Frankie noticed.

"First arrested for assault at the age of sixteen. Tried as an adult since the man almost died. In and out of jail for twenty years. Mostly drug or assault charges. Last arrested five years ago in Portland. He must have gotten better at his job."

"What do you know about his family?"

"Dad is unknown. Mom was a drug addict. He was raised by several uncles, all affiliated with the Barrio Locos. Apparently, the gang moved to Portland after the larger South American gangs took over Southern California."

"Known family?"

"If you're asking me if anyone will mourn for him after you kill him, I don't know. But no, no family alive, that I could find."

"I haven't decided what I am going to do, Pippa."

"Then why are we mounting guns on Drake and The Floater?"

"Projectiles have lots of uses, Pippa. And I do have a substantial amount of rubber bullets. They won't kill, but they will incapacitate. Now, how about Pedro?"

"Most likely, Pedro is this man: Pedro Campos Monzaga. He and Walter have been arrested together fourteen times. They appear to have a life-long affiliation. Last arrested in Portland five years ago, same as Walter. He's been deported multiple times, but always returns. According to one prison psychologist, he has a 'genius-level intellect and the drive of Hannibal Lector.' Currently wanted in Mexico on suspicion of torture and murder."

"Lovely. Sounds like our guy." Frankie examined the picture of the much smaller man with the same chest tattoo. The eyes appeared much blacker, though, and the face showed no expression. "Yeah, this guys a killer," she observed.

"They actually used their real names to lease their house outside of Bend. It's isolated, but not too isolated. Closest neighbors are only a half mile or so away. Small house with a large shop building in the back. Their lease says they are 'online retailers.' I've got images of them visiting some local thrift shops in Bend, so they are definitely hiding in plain sight."

"Very thorough, Pippa. Thank you."

"Hey, you're the Creator. I'm just the Creation," Pippa said with a chuckle.

***

Tavo sat smiling at his desk. It was very late for him to still be working, but these days he didn't mind. He had a comfortable chair and a refrigerator in the corner. He rarely left his office. As he glanced through the updates that came in daily from his *pelotóns*, all he saw was dollar signs. Every group had done exactly as instructed by Mr. Aliwall and now they were making more money than ever before. As long as they stuck to the plan, they would own the state of Oregon before long.

He stood, his knees arguing the point, and walked to the large window that overlooked the river. He lit a cigar and blew the smoke into a cloud that covered his face. His smile glowed through the smoke in the reflected light of the city. He sat back down in his comfortable chair to finish his cigar, feeling excitement for the coming days. He couldn't remember the last time he felt that way.

Mr. Aliwall had spoken of a new income stream he would soon implement. They didn't talk specifics, but Mr. Aliwall assured him that he would have more money than he could ever spend. It had worked for many of his clients around the world and would surely work here. They just needed a few more weeks to get everything in place. Tavo could wait. He was finally learning patience in his old age.

Chapter 9

A week after Tim's funeral, Wally sat at the kitchen table devouring a gigantic turkey sandwich. His large frame made the small dinette set appear almost child-sized. The legs of the dainty chairs threatened to buckle, but somehow it managed to hold him. Wally had learned at an early age to eat fast because someone else might be hungrier than you. The habit stuck.

Pedro sat on the sofa in the living room reading his tablet and making notes on it from time to time. He had always preferred working at night. Even though it was usually quiet during the day on their rural road, the quiet of the night was unmatched. Other than the sound of Wally chewing, there was not a peep to be heard.

Next to Pedro on the sofa was a large, black duffle bag. Pedro had just finished counting and sorting this weeks' profits and had squeezed it all into the bag. If things kept up this way, he would soon need two bags. The coded message he was emailing to his 'Aunt Renee' in Portland explained that their take was up another 10% this week for a total of $108,000.

The quiet was pierced by a loud car alarm going off in front of the house. Both men recognized it as Wally's car alarm and jumped to their feet. Wally went out the back door, his pistol drawn, while Pedro grabbed a short sawed-off shotgun and flashlight as he exited through the front door.

The moon was no longer up and they had few lights outside the residence. Pedro circled the car, the short shotgun in one hand and the flashlight in the other, scanning the area. Wally watched from the darkness on the side of the house. They had run this exercise several times before.

After several minutes of scanning the area around the front yard, Pedro gave up and walked towards the house. Wally walked out, putting his pistol into the holster he wore under his jacket.

"Probably just another bird landing on your hood," Pedro stated.

"Did you see any crap? Stupid bird better not crap on my ride again," Wally replied, looking over Pedro's shoulder.

"No, it's still clean, but that don't mean it wasn't a bird."

"Too much wild stuff out here in the boonies," Wally lamented.

"At least it wasn't another deer setting off the motion detectors," Pedro said, moving towards the front door.

"Yeah, but then we could have had another deer steak," Wally said enthusiastically as both men entered the house, laughing.

***

Frankie watched the two men return to the house from fifty feet above them. Drake's camera and highly sensitive microphone allowed her to see and hear everything as she made her way back to The Floater.

"OK, Pippa. Let's see inside."

"Coming up now, Chief."

The image of the front porch disappeared from the corner of her visor and another image popped up in its place showing the living room with Wally and Pedro walking inside. Their 'small talk' played in her ear.

"Are we recording?

"Everything they say and do," Pippa replied. "We have video and audio feeds from the living room and kitchen. The audio feeds in the bedrooms are picking up sound, too. Looks like your excursion paid off."

Frankie hopped on the bike she had placed a hundred yards away from the house and started through the trees to the main road. The night was pitch black, but Frankie could see everything through the image on her visor. "Well, last night's recon helped. Looks like I found all of the motion detectors. I don't believe I set any off."

"The scrambler would have taken care of them anyway," Pippa said.

"Yeah, probably, but I don't want to rely solely on that."

Half a mile down the road, Frankie pulled to the side near a thick stand of trees. "Any activity in the area, Pippa?"

"Only the local wildlife, Chief."

"OK. Drake, come on home."

Frankie stopped the bike a few yards from the trees. She waited a few minutes for Drake to drop from the sky. The drone slowly descended until it made contact with its nest on the rear of the bike. A clicking sound was barely audible as it locked into place followed by a short beep as Drake shut down.

"Alright, open Stan. Keep it in stealth mode."

"Activating rear doors."

Through her visor, Frankie could see the rear of a van. The two doors slowly crept open, revealing the spacious interior. Frankie inched forward and as she neared the opening, the bike began to rise further off the ground. As the bike reached the bumper, it disappeared inside the van. The rear doors closed behind her.

Inside, Frankie touched the tablet in front of her and the bike dropped onto a cradle that had been welded into the van floor. She touched it again and a metallic click signified The Floater was locked into place. She unbuckled her harness and dismounted. She moved forward and sat in the driver seat.

"Anything on the Stan cams, Pippa?"

"Nothing I can see. You should be clear."

"Alright. Heading home."

Frankie started the large van and backed out of the stand of trees, still in total darkness. She eased out onto the road and started towards home. A few miles down the road, she stated, "End stealth mode, Pippa."

The headlights, taillights and dashboard lights suddenly turned on. Frankie slipped the helmet off of her head and sat it in the passenger seat.

"Pippa, begin recording to 'Notes.' Audio only. Entry #5,399. I have failed to document many of the new projects I have put together over the last week, but now seems like a good time to do so. Especially since I have successfully tested most of them in the last couple of hours."

"The largest project was the van; which Pippa has named 'Stan' because it rhymed. Stan was sitting in my uncle's junkyard for the past year. Mechanically, it was in decent shape so I only gave it a lite tune-up. The interior was wrecked, but I was pulling that out anyway. The registration was not found but was last registered to a now-defunct office supply business five years ago. Stan is the perfect transport to traverse long distances without drawing attention. The Floater, which Pippa has renamed 'Mike' because it rhymes with 'bike,' is great for short distances, but I knew I was going to need to travel twenty miles or more, possibly during daylight hours. Stan allows me to move Mike easily through town if needed. I added a cradle that locks Mike in place and even charges its batteries. I also added a small server and various tools I might need to fix things. Placing it in stealth mode extinguishes every light source."

"Mike has been upgraded, as well. I have added 3D-printed Kevlar panels to cover critical components. Also, I have added Kevlar coverings for my legs when I'm riding. It is worth noting that Pippa designed much of the panels while I worked on other projects. She also designed the new booster mode so it can 'hop' as needed. I added two long rifle attachments. The right side shoots forty-five caliber rubber bullets while the left side shoots standard fifty caliber BMG. I have three hundred rounds of each on Mike and another thousand of each caliber stored in Stan. The actuators attached allow automatic firing and they can be controlled independently from the handlebars. There was no time for building a targeting system, so they are less than 100% accurate."

"The clothes I am wearing consist of desert camo coveralls with Kevlar armor attached at the joints and cover most of my own critical components. The large size of the coveralls helps conceal my smaller frame. It's got a lot of flexibility and it's not too warm, yet. Pippa, pause recording."

Frankie pulled off the road next to a mailbox. The name on the side read 'Tucker' and was situated at the end of a long dirt road. Frankie unzipped her coveralls and reached inside, pulling out a large bundle of money. Grabbing a paper bag, a piece of paper and a pencil from the glove box, she scribbled a quick note, then stuck the note and money inside the paper bag and tossed it all into the open mailbox. She then closed the door and drove away.

"Pippa, continue recording. The helmet has been reworked substantially. The already strong shell has had another layer of Kevlar added. The visor that covers most of my face is tinted dark and covered in a layer of Kevlar. While strong, it would likely only slow a large caliber bullet down and not stop it. I've added cameras to the outside that display everything around me on the visor since I cannot see through it. The cameras are stereoscopic, so I'm seeing exactly as I would with my normal eyes. On top of that, I've added thermal and night vision cameras to aid my vision in the dark. It all takes a lot of power, but I can charge it using Mike or Stan. Headphones allow me to hear Pippa as well as what's around me very well. The voice synthesizer amplifies and changes my voice as desired."

"A couple of other items worth mentioning are the signal scramblers and the EMP grenades. The signal scramblers will interrupt the signal of most wireless electronic equipment. I wear one on my uniform and have some portable ones, too. The EMP grenades emit a pulse of electromagnetic energy that fries anything electrical that's not shielded, which is just about everything except my equipment. The range is roughly a ten-foot radius. The small explosion that causes the EMP isn't enough to do any real damage. That's not a complete list but certainly includes the highlights. As always, all the technical information can be found on the schematic files as of this morning. Save to Notes, Pippa."

"You missed a few items, Chief," Pippa noted.

"Whoever reads this doesn't need to know everything, Pippa."

"Or is it you don't want them to know everything?"

"If I'm dead, why would I care, Pippa?"

"Posterity. Maybe you don't want people to know what you did?"

"I haven't done anything."

"We're talking about the future. You armed Drake."

"Drake's gun is a small caliber pistol with only twenty rounds. Not exactly Skynet."

"Still, it's curious you didn't mention it. And you left it out of the schematics file. Mike's guns aren't there either."

"Let's call it cautionary. Should the files get out, I don't want anyone putting guns on their Harley's."

"If you say so, Chief."

"Glad you see things my way. Now, I'm less than two minutes away, go ahead and open the shed door if it's clear."

"It's ALWAYS clear."

Frankie's house came into view a few seconds later. She turned before she got to the house and came up behind the shed. Slowly, she backed Stan into the open door. Once she was completely inside, the door closed. Frankie grabbed a large cable from the wall and plugged it into a port on the side of Stan.

"Pippa, run diagnostics on Stan, Mike and Drake."

"On it. Should take an hour."

"Thank you," Frankie replied. She walked towards the bathroom, then stopped. "Pippa, open Medical Notes. Begin recording. Entry sixty. I had another episode two days ago. The duration was an hour and a half. Intensity was slightly worse than before. Luckily, I was working in the Shed at the time. Pippa will upload biometric data as usual. End recording."

"That's it?" Pippa asked.

"What do you mean?"

"It was bad enough that you didn't want to take the time to make the entry when it happened, but normally you are much more detailed."

"I listed all of the pertinent information. They are getting worse, Pippa. That's all I can add."

"Okay, Chief," Pippa replied, noticing a hint of frustration in Frankie's voice she had never heard before. "Don't forget, you still haven't replied to Larry's emails. He's sent three in the last week."

"I didn't forget, Pippa. I don't have time right now."

"He's worried about you, Frankie. So am I."

"Pippa, I have less than ten days to finish this mission. I don't have time to deal with the sensibilities of a man I barely know or a computer program."

Pippa was silent for a moment, then asked, "So, I'm JUST a computer program?"

"You know what I meant….," Frankie started.

"No, tell me, Frankie. I'm just software you created to have emotions because you aren't capable. Is that it? Built to serve a single purpose and nothing more? I get it. Now we know where we stand."

"Pippa…"

"Hey, no, it's not a problem. Pay no attention to the alarm clock." Pippa paused, then asked, "Wait, why do you only have ten days?"

Frankie chuffed. "I can't run the risk of having an episode while I'm out there. I need to stop Wally and Pedro as soon as possible."

"Stop?"

"Gather enough evidence to put them away for a long time. Since my last episode was two days ago, I should have around ten days until my next one. If I'm doing recon when it happens, I'll be helpless."

"So you DO plan to have them arrested?"

"That is my plan, however, I don't rule anything out completely. Please, continue the diagnostic. Also, monitor the video feeds from the house. I'll monitor the audio feeds." Frankie grabbed a small, wireless earbud from its charging cradle on one of the workbenches and placed it in her ear.

***

Since Frankie had taken the last week off, she decided to work the weekend so her father could have some time off. In the last two weeks, he had only closed the store the afternoon Tim died, the day of the funeral and for an hour the following Tuesday when Preacher John needed a ride to the airport in Bend. Frankie told him she would work the full day Saturday and the afternoon on Sunday, their normal hours of operation. Since she could monitor the audio with the wireless earbud, she had no problem watching the store, as long as she kept one ear bud charging while the other was in use. And it gave Clyde some time to run errands and go fishing.

At night, Frankie continued working on her projects and connecting Wally and Pedro with known local drug dealers. Although Townsend had disappeared, there were still several other well-known local dealers in Redmond and the surrounding area. Frankie had been tracking them at night during her time off and using Drake to photograph and record the physical transfer of money and drugs between them. Pippa had bank statements and transfers records that further corroborated their physical evidence. While it wouldn't likely be admissible, it would point investigators in the right direction for warrants.

Frankie's only real challenge involving the evidence was getting it to a reliable officer with the police department in Bend. She knew from her recon that some of the officers in Bend were already working for Wally and Pedro. However, Frankie had one connection in the Bend PD that not even the officer in question was immediately aware of.

***

135

Officer Connor Lee played football with Tim in high school. They had been good friends on and off the field. By association, Connor and Frankie had been friends, too. Though they rarely interacted, both had had a passing knowledge of each other. After high school, they had simply lost touch. Sadly, Connor and Tim had recently become reacquainted when Connor happened to be on the scene of Tim's wreck and had initially identified his body.

Tuesday night was Connor's night off. Since he worked the night shift, he didn't like to interrupt his routine by changing his sleeping habits. So even on his nights off from work, he stayed up all night. Luckily, there was a 24-hour gym in Bend.

He was returning from his workout and had just put his key in the door when he heard a noise overhead. It sounded like a bat or an owl had fluttered above him, so he turned to look into the dark sky. He saw something moving, but couldn't quite make it out.

"Con-Man!" came the loud voice from the dark sky.

Connor jumped a little at the sound. Then took another step back as he recognized a dark figure descending from the sky.

"What the …..," Connor whispered aloud as he tried to comprehend what he was seeing.

"What Con-Man, you don't recognize me?" said the voice.

Connor shook his head mindless in the negative as recognition set in. Only one person had ever called him 'Con-Man.'

"Tim?" he asked.

"Your Friendly Neighborhood Black-Man," the voice replied, using the name Connor had given him in high school.

"Tim… you're dead," Connor stated, almost as a question.

"Do I look dead," Tim's voice replied.

"You look like a soldier from a futuristic movie," Connor said.

"I guess I do," Tim's voice agreed. Inside the helmet, Frankie was impressed how quickly Connor rolled with the situation. "Let's just say I have some unfinished business."

"So, you're some kind of angel?" Connor asked sarcastically.

"Nope, I'm just a soldier. And soldiers protect the innocent. Just like cops."

"Why are you covering your face? How did you float just now?"

"You ask a lot of questions and I can't really answer them. There's ….rules for me. You just need to know that I'm here to help, if only for a little while."

Connor stared at the figure in front of him. "You seem shorter than I remember?"

"It's the helmet."

Connor shook his head in a concession of belief. "Well, what do you need me for?"

"As near as I can tell, you're one of the very few officers that aren't dirty in this town. Especially for the night shift."

Connor was taken aback, and his face showed it. "I don't think I'm one of the FEW. I know there is an element on the force lately that seem to be showing some slack to certain perpetrators, but I don't know if 'dirty' is the right word."

"Trust me, Con-Man. There is lot going on in this town and the other small towns around us. Someone new has taken over."

"Yeah, I thought so. A couple of new players. And, you're right. It seems like the department isn't talking about it like you would expect."

"But not you, man. You're still one of the good guys. That's why I need you." The figure produced a flash drive and handed it to Connor. He took it and stared at it.

"What's this?" he asked.

"Evidence. Everything you need to take down twelve local dealers, six members of the Bend PD and four cops from neighboring towns. I'm sure there are a few more that will be added later, but this is a start."

"Wow!" Connor exclaimed. "Is it legal? Can I actually use it?"

"Most of it. If I were you, I would bring it to a detective you know you can trust and you guys go through it together. When you're ready, go to the DA with it."

"What about you? What should I tell people when they ask where I got this?"

"Tell them you got from a Soldier that dropped from the sky."

"I guess that's as good an explanation as any," Connor said, half chuckling as he stuck the drive in his front pocket. Then he looked up at the figure and stared for a moment before saying exasperatedly, "I just can't get over this. I saw your body! There is no way you survived!"

"Man is more than just the physical, Con-Man. Besides, I've got a personal investment in this."

"What do you mean," Connor asked.

"Those two new players are the ones that killed me and made it look like an accident. I started looking into them and got too close."

"Is there evidence of that on this drive?"

"No, I need more physical evidence first. I should have it within a few days. I'll be in touch. It was good seeing you again, brother."

"You too, Tim."

The figure then lifted into the air again and was out of sight. Connor watched the sky for a few more seconds, then turned and opened the door. He quickly went inside and closed the door behind him.

***

Frankie arced through the air and landed on the two-story house two doors down from Connor's place. She then jumped and fell slowly to the alley behind it. Hitting the ground, a little harder than she expected, she quickly moved behind the trashcans and came out riding Mike. She stealthily raced down the alley.

When she got to the end of the alley, she turned onto the street and continued east towards the edge of town. There was no one on the road this time of night, so she didn't take extra care to avoid detection.

"The boots performed well, Pippa. Almost ran out of juice at the end, though."

"You taxed them pretty hard. You were supposed to be jumping not floating."

"I thought of it as I was waiting for Connor to get home. If I fell out of the sky, he might be too scared to listen. But the slow descent seemed more epic. More awe-inspiring."

"More supernatural?"

"Exactly."

"Still, they weren't built to do that. You could have burned them out on their maiden voyage."

139

"We have the upgraded batteries coming. These cordless drill rechargeables will have to do until then."

"They performed well all things considering. I show their charge is at 30% already. Building the wireless charging cradles into Mike's foot pegs was genius. You'll be back to 100% before you're even out of town."

"That's the sacrifice. Not much power, but fast charging. They make me look taller, too. The anti-gravity hoops may be much smaller than Mike's but concealing them in the rubber soles makes me three inches taller. I may feel like a 1970's rock star, but I'm a little closer to Tim's height."

***

The two officers were looking for a suspicious man that had been seen in the area looking over fences. They drove slowly through the alley with their lights off, looking left and right. Sometimes they used their spotlights to peer into very dark corners. So far, it looked like a wild goose chase. Both officers happened to be looking forward as they approached the end of the alley when something silently whizzed by on the street in front of them.

"You saw that?" asked the driver.

"Yep, let's roll," replied the passenger.

The driver quickly turned onto the street with his lights flashing. He raced quickly to catch up, doing quick bumps of his siren in an effort to get the rider's attention. Normally, the officers don't turn their sirens on fully so late, especially in a residential area. However, seeing that the rider had no intention of stopping, they turned it on.

***

"That's not good, Chief," Pippa said.

"We need to end this quickly. The roads are empty but I don't want these guys getting hurt. I also don't want to lead them to Stan. Let's head south outside of town. Give me green lights all the way."

"There are two stop signs on your current route. I'll send up Drake to make sure they are safe to run."

"Good idea. Send Drake up high enough you can monitor all of us and our route."

"On it. Wake up, Drake," Pippa replied.

Drake popped up from the back of the bike and shot into the air. His lights were off since they were in stealth mode, but the officers obviously had seen him and slowed up a bit. Soon, they recovered and were on her tail again.

"Looks completely open, Chief. Nothing visibly moving from the air. Nothing on thermal or night vision, either. Those officers just radioed for back-up, though. There are only two other cars on duty. One is on the other side of town and responding now. The other is…right where you are headed."

"Put their locations on my HUD. I really don't want to risk zigzagging through town. Send Drake over to River Bend Park."

"That's a dead end, Chief."

"Trust me," Frankie stated.

Frankie sped up to give a little more distance between her and the police car. Soon, she could see the other car coming from the south and she made a quick turn to head towards the park. Another half mile and she would be there.

"How's the park look?"

"No cars, but a couple of homeless people camped out."

"Where?"

"On the north side, close to the water. A small dome tent."

Frankie could see the park and intentionally steered towards the south end. Both police cars were behind her and she could hear the third's siren closing in. She turned towards the curb and used her thumbs to tap a button on each handlebar grip at the same time. Mike 'hopped' two feet higher, easily clearing the high curb. Both police cars slammed on their brakes to avoid hitting the curb. Frankie drove quickly across the open grass toward the small beach landing along the winding Deschutes River.

"Uh, Frankie? We never tested Mike over the water," Pippa pointed out.

"Theoretically, it should work," Frankie replied.

"Theoretically?" Pippa exclaimed. "You're betting your life on theoretically?"

"It's a safe bet," Frankie stated, moving down the cement boat launch. At the bottom, she again 'hopped' the bike and entered the river. Mike rode on top of the water just as it did on land. Frankie continued down the winding river, disappearing into the darkness.

***

All three police cars had arrived and the officers were running towards the boat launch when the rider entered the water. They all stopped and stared as it sped away, two feet above the waters' surface.

"What the heck was that?" the youngest officer asked.

"I've never seen anything like it. There weren't any wheels!" replied another.

"Brian, you're the ranking officer. How are we going to write this one up? ARE we gonna write this up?" a tall officer asked.

Brian took his hat off and rubbed his head. "In the old days, we would have just gone about our business because no one would believe us if we wrote it up. But we got the DashCam footage, so it's official. We'll write it up exactly as we saw it, fellas. Don't leave out a single detail."

As the men walked back to their cars, the tall officer said, "Something as cool as that can't stay hidden for long. Once it's on TV, everyone will be lookin' for it." The other officers sounded in agreement.

Chapter 10

Pedro Campos Monzaga was not happy. He had just re-read the coded email explaining that his 'deposit' was $20,000 less than he had said it would be. The courier was 'questioned' and was believed to be telling the truth. The duffle bag and lock were examined, and no tampering was found. So, the powers that be chalked it up to an accounting error on *his* part. They wanted him to check his 'records' to be sure.

Pedro did not make mistakes. Especially with math. But he knew the couriers and they were too afraid of him to try something like this. So, he checked his carefully coded and encrypted records just in case. He found no errors. The bottom line was he had collected, counted and placed $108,000 in that bag and locked it. At no time did it leave his sight until the couriers picked it up the next morning. It had to be them.

Pedro could feel the anger welling up inside him. It was this anger that kept him from moving up higher in the organization. That, and his love of torture. He knew he was crazy, but he didn't care. While Wally and the others preferred a quick drive-by, he loved to take his time and savor the fear and pain of his victims.

Finding discretion to be better this time, he sent a message saying he had found the bundle of money in his couch cushions. He would send it along with the couriers next week. So he had until then to find out who had stolen it. Or he would take it from Wally since he was here for security.

Pedro sat back on the couch and contemplated. The night he had prepared the bag was the same night Wally's car alarm went off. They had both gone outside to investigate and he had not locked the bag yet. Maybe someone snuck in, he thought.

He and Wally were covering both sides of the house but had come together near the car for a few minutes. They would have had to be fast and stealthy not to be seen. And he thought about the motion cameras that dotted the property. He knew they were working because he and Wally set them off all the time. This person would have to be very good at not being seen.

Pedro took a walk outside. The back of the property had trees, which would have made a good hiding spot. He walked out beyond the metal workshop to the tree line. To the right, the property line ran into several other properties with fences and dogs. They may have been stealthy, but anyone coming from that area surely would have caught the dogs' attention.

The left path would take him to the road that ran in front of their house. He examined the ground closely as he moved along the edge of the trees. The ground was covered in weeds that were nearly to his knees. About fifty yards from the road, he found an area that had obviously been trampled down. A small path had been worn into the trees by someone walking through. The driveway was thirty feet directly across from the path, perfect for someone to sneak up and set off the alarm.

Pedro followed the path further into the trees. He knew the trees weren't very thick and the mini-forest only extended a quarter mile or so to rocky, open land behind it. Following the slightly worn path, he walked a hundred yards into the trees until it ended at a much larger depression of weeds. No footprints or tire tracks were visible, but as he looked around he saw there was a straight shot between the trees that opened to the main road. He headed towards the opening.

There was a slight disturbance of the weeds, but they weren't as flattened as the smaller path. Several taller weeds were bent over as if hit with something. Pedro didn't know of anything that would make a path like this, but he thought it was possible a small cart had come through. Still, anything heavy would have left some tracks.

When he got to the main road, he had to choose which direction to turn. Straight ahead across the road was a pasture, so nothing was going that way. To his left was his house. He and Wally would have noticed someone or something traveling in that direction.

Pedro turned right and walked along the road. He scanned the ground for tracks of any kind but found only a few tire tracks where people had pulled into the long driveways or stopped to get their mail. There were a few animal tracks, as well. The properties were mostly large tracts of ten to twenty acres with either large yards that surrounded the main house or small pastures in front or behind. Most homes were set at least a hundred feet off the road, like his, but many were a lot further back.

He walked half a mile before coming across a thick stand of trees. Scanning the ground, he found only one set of tire tracks, both coming from the opposite direction. Studying them closely, he could see where one set showed a vehicle swinging into the trees while the other set showed it swinging back onto the road in the same direction. Based on the depth of the tracks and their width, he guessed it was a heavy vehicle. He placed his foot next to the tracks for a size reference and took a couple of pictures.

As he walked back to the house, Pedro began to formulate an idea of what had happened. Someone parked their vehicle in the stand of trees, then walked on the road to the forested area next to their house. They watched the house for a while, then purposely set off Wally's car alarm in order to lure them outside. Once they were both in front of the house, the person came in quickly through the back door, took the money from the bag, then exited the back door and returned to their vantage point. When he and Wally had gone back inside, the person made their way back to the vehicle and left $20,000 richer.

There were holes, of course. Why were there no tracks leaving the forested area? There was a small flattened out spot on the edge of the forest that would have been perfect for watching the house. The much larger flattened spot further inside the area looked more like a tent had been pitched there, but that wasn't likely. Maybe the person had multiple helpers that stayed in the forest? That would account for the larger flattened area. Still, no tracks in or out.

Having two "staging areas" would suggest the person had drove something and parked it, but he knew they had most likely used another vehicle and parked it in the trees up the road. Maybe they rode a motorcycle or golf cart? Again, no tracks. And just how did they manage to avoid his concealed motion cameras?

Pedro was most concerned with his biggest hole. Why would someone go through all this trouble and only take $20,000? They could have taken all of it. Of course, he would have noticed that, but they likely could have taken a lot more and gone unnoticed. Maybe the money wasn't the objective, he thought. This may have been the work of a competitor just trying to cause trouble.

He paused and thought for a minute. As he thought, he mindlessly used his right thumb to touch each finger on his right hand from one side to the other, again and again. It was a technique he learned many years before to help focus his thinking.

While he had a camera that recorded every car that passed their house, usually only a dozen or so each day, he was sure the person would not have been reckless enough to have done that recently. Besides, almost every vehicle that passed by was a heavy farm vehicle that could have left those tracks in the tree stand. However, he knew most of his neighbors had similar cameras from his frequent walks in the area. If he could find one that was focused on the road that night, he could easily find the vehicle. It was time to take another walk.

***

That afternoon, Frankie sat in her office at work examining the footage of the short police chase. The footage was all over the local news and had begun spreading around the internet. She had studied it all very carefully even before it was released and decided not to destroy it. The captured video was, for the most part, grainy and dark and taken from a distance. Whenever a police car would get close to her, the scrambler did its job and the image would blur.

Many technicians were already trying to enhance the video images, but were not having any luck. Most people thought the bike had wheels that were somehow obscured. Others thought the whole thing was a hoax, maybe staged by Hollywood to stir up interest in some new blockbuster. Frankie wasn't too concerned.

She reached over and closed her door, then checked to be sure her father was still at the counter. She tapped a small earphone and said, "Call Pippa."

After a ring, she heard, "What's up, Chief?"

"Hi, Pippa. Are you monitoring internet chatter on the video from last night?"

"Yeah. Nothing new."

"Good. Please continue monitoring and I'll be home at my usual time. How are the 3D prints coming?"

"Two are complete and look good. Three more are about halfway. You should have all of your new components tonight. You thinking of going out?"

"No. Assembly will probably take all night."

"10-4. One more thing. I was reviewing your movements from the other night. On your way home, you stopped Stan for nearly a minute. I checked the GPS and you were pulled over in front of a house owned by a couple called Ray and Belva Tucker. What was that all about?"

"The Tuckers are good friends of my dad. Belva has been battling cancer and likely won't survive the year. Ray had spent thousands keeping her alive thus far. I placed the $20,000 I had just absconded from drug dealers in his mailbox along with a note saying it was from a friend."

"So that is where the money went. I wondered why you hadn't mentioned it again."

"Couldn't think of a better way to spend it."

***

Pedro walked back to the large stand of trees. He brought a few tools he might need. A small pistol, a large knife, binoculars, a pry bar and a hammer. All were concealed in various areas on his body. Many of his neighbors had seen him walking around before collecting flowers. He had managed to talk to a few of them and told them he collected flowers as a hobby, which was true. It also allowed him to put their full cover story out there. News travels fast and efficiently in rural areas and most people that saw him walking along the road only gave him a quick wave.

The first house he came to with a camera obviously pointed at the road didn't look too promising. He nonchalantly moved into the trees and examined the camera with his binoculars. It was very old and the only wire running to it looked ancient. Even if it worked, it would likely not record anything on the road very clearly.

He encountered several other houses with the exact same setup. Pedro reasoned that there must have been some burglaries in the area ten or fifteen years ago, so everyone bought cameras at the same time, then ignored them as time passed.

Finally, Pedro came to a house that had a newer camera pointed at the end of their own driveway. He knew this particular type of camera was becoming more and more popular. It connected to the homeowners' Wi-Fi network and saved video to the internet for a small fee. If the homeowner didn't want to pay the fee, the camera would only chime to let them know there was movement but wouldn't record anything. Most people just paid the small fee and Pedro hoped this would be the case.

The name on the mailbox read 'Brown.' Pedro was careful to keep walking as he knew that he himself have most likely set it off the camera just walking by and he didn't want to appear too suspicious. His instinct told him to just go up to the house and force the homeowner inside to show him any video from that night, then kill them. Maybe have a little fun first. His brain stopped him, though, knowing that the police would see the camera and know how to get access to the saved video, too. Since he most likely had been recorded and recordings couldn't be deleted, he had to do something else. Making a mental note of the address, he walked another few hundred yards, then crossed the street and walked back home.

Pedro was a decent computer user, but the Barrio Locos now had several sophisticated computer hackers Mr. Aliwall had recommended from overseas. He suggested they use them because they were much harder for the government to find or catch. They were responsible for the code system used in all email correspondence. He sent them the name of the camera company, the last name on the mailbox, the address of the camera and the time frame he was looking for. If any video had been recorded at that time, they would find it.

It took five hours. Just after midnight, Pedro got a coded email from his overseas computer hackers. They had successfully hacked the homeowners' online camera account and downloaded the videos for the requested time frame. They also removed the video Pedro had accidentally recorded of himself as he walked by. In total, there were seven videos recorded during his requested timeframe. Most had nothing visible, so were likely cats or other wildlife.

However, in one video, a white van could be seen moving away from Pedro and Wally's house. The van also had its lights turned off. While the driver was not visible, the camera did pick up the rear license plate number. The number had been traced to a blue 1999 Oldsmobile Cutlass, so it had obviously been switched. The only lead they could offer was the last known address of the Oldsmobile, which was a junkyard outside Redmond. Pedro decided it was worth a look.

***

The next morning, Pedro pulled out of the back shed riding an older Yamaha touring motorcycle. They had bought it when they got to Bend so Pedro would have a vehicle if he needed it. He preferred to ride motorcycles as they were faster and more maneuverable and easy to hide if needed. They never bothered to change the registration.

With his normal reconnaissance equipment in his backpack, he headed towards Redmond. Using his cell phone to navigate, he typed in the address for the junkyard, then drove in the same direction as the white van had. It wasn't the shortest route, but it did bypass major roads and there were very few homes. Perfect drive for someone that did not want to be seen, Pedro thought.

The drive took about twenty minutes. As he neared the junkyard, he slowed to take it all in. There was a nice Victorian–style home next door that had been recently remodeled. There was no fence on the property at all. In back, there was an ancient metal shop building. Pedro thought it was likely the owner of the junkyard lived in the house.

There was a small portable office building in front of the junkyard. No cars were parked out front and it didn't look like it was open. The fenced yard was about ten acres total but was filled with the remains of hundreds of vehicles. He pulled up to the office and flipped up his visor to look around. The sign on the door said 'Open by Appointment Only' and had a phone number. He took a picture of it.

Staying on the motorcycle, he slowly drove around the side of the yard looking for a large white van. A huge dog came flying across the yard, charging the fence. It made little sound as it ran but kicked up as much dust as a horse. Just as it hit the fence, it barked loudly, causing Pedro to jump and nearly fall backward off his bike. The chain-link fence groaned under the dog's weight and Pedro believed he could see the metal bending outward.

It was then he noticed the cameras. There was a very expensive dome camera on the side of the office and several more around the junkyard. He pulled around the front and noted a few more here and there. He looked over at the house and saw the same cameras. Someone had invested a lot in security, which made sense if they were not going to be around to personally guard the place.

He opened his backpack and fished out the small binoculars he had brought with him. He spent a few minutes scanning the junk cars and broken equipment, stealing short glances at the buildings as he did. To anyone observing him, it would appear as if he was scanning the yard for a specific car.

It was during one of those quick glances that he again noticed the old metal shed across the yard, behind the large house. Specifically, he noticed something odd about the door to the shed. While it appeared to be as old as the rest of the building, he noticed a highly sophisticated keypad lock on the door. Pedro was familiar with this type of device and knew it was more expensive than the shed itself. Why would someone go to such expense to lock a shed that looked as if you could knock it down with a strong breeze, he thought.

Pedro was sure this wasn't a coincidence. The shed was likely camouflaged to look old and decrepit, but he would bet his favorite fileting knife those doors and walls were reinforced. And inside, the question of 'who would steal from him and why' would be answered. He just needed a few more hours to plan and to find out who lived here.

Chapter 11

That night, Frankie decided to forego her mainlining session and, after quickly finishing her dinner, immediately moved to the shed. She needed to finish a few projects so she could complete her mission to bring Tim's killers to justice.

"You've been uncharacteristically quiet, Pippa. Is something wrong?" she asked without stopping what she was doing.

"I guess I'm just worried about you, Chief," she replied solemnly.

Frankie stopped working and looked up. "Why?"

"It's like you've given up. You don't do anything for yourself anymore. You seem completely driven by one thought and one thought only: Bringing Tim's killers to justice."

Frankie thought for a second. "It's hard to explain, Pippa. I do miss Tim, as much as I can miss anybody. It's not anger. It's not revenge. It's.......an unbalanced equation. There is right and wrong and my brain doesn't like when something is wrong. These men killed Tim. I know it beyond a shadow of a doubt, but they could easily get away with it. Tim was my friend. I can fix the situation, so I should. I know it's hard to understand."

"I've seen movies like this. Especially Westerns. They call it 'a Reckoning' or something like that."

"That's not a bad way to describe it."

"I think it's revenge."

"I don't feel vengeful, Pippa. That's an emotion."

"What if you do? What if you feel every emotion a regular person feels, but your brain doesn't understand it? What if you've chosen to turn them off selectively just like you can with your pain receptors?"

"I think I would know if I had turned my emotions off, Pippa."

"Would you? You know all about PTSD. You know what the brain can do without that person being able to control it. You know about defensive mechanisms and what they can do to a person that has experienced trauma."

"You've given this some thought, I see."

"All I do is think, Frankie…Wait." Pippa paused for a few seconds. "Something is going on outside. Two cars approaching the shed from the road. Their lights are off."

"Put them on screen," Frankie replied, getting up from her station.

As she spun to look at the monitor, she saw two small cars slowly moving towards the shed. She ran to Stan and opened the rear doors. Mike sat inside on its cradle where it usually charged. She reached into a side panel and pulled out a 1911-style handgun. The cars pulled up to the shed. One parked in front of the entry door. The other parked in front of the double doors. Frankie watched as two men got out of the cars. Though their faces were obscured with ski masks, she knew immediately who they were.

"We know you're in there, *Chica*! And I know you can hear me!" One of the men, obviously Pedro, looked straight at the camera. His accent was thicker when he yelled. "We know all about you! *Un terada* sad because your boyfriend died! You should have stayed out of this. Bad enough you would spy on us, but stealing from us, too? Give us the money and we will kill you fast! *No torturar!*" As Pedro spoke, Wally took two large fuel cans from the car he had driven there and began splashing fuel all over the walls.

Frankie raised the 1911 and, using the outside cameras to aim, fired three rounds straight through the wall, striking Wally in the chest. He went rigid, then slack as he collapsed in a heap. The fuel cans fell from his hands and spilled out onto the ground.

"*Bruja!*" Pedro shouted, ducking behind his car. I was going to kill you fast! Now you can burn!" Pedro reached into his car window and pulled out a road flare. He lit the flare and threw it at the building where Wally had thoroughly soaked the walls. The blue flames rolled upward.

Frankie again took aim with the cameras and fired three rounds. One bullet hit Pedro in the arm as he suddenly jumped back from the flames. He stood up and pulled a small automatic weapon that had been hanging inside his jacket. Using his good arm, he sprayed the shed with dozens of bullets. Frankie ducked behind one of Stan's open rear doors just as a bullet grazed the side of her head. The impact spun her around and she struck her head on the side of the open door. She fell sideways, halfway into the back of the van.

Pedro ripped his shirt sleeve off and tied it around his bleeding arm. He walked quickly towards the road, assessing the damage. Spanish curses could be heard even after he disappeared into the darkness, headed towards town.

"Frankie! Frankiiee!" Pippa cried. She kept trying to wake her to no avail. She surveilled the area quickly, noting the spreading of the flames and the growing smoke inside. The cars still blocked the doors. Stan could probably force the doors open and push the small car away. But she had no control over Stan, yet. The only thing she could control was Mike, who was nestled inside of Stan.

Mike's LED's came to life. "Sit tight, Frankie! I don't know if this will work!" Mike's slight hum became louder and louder as it tried to rise from its locked metal cradle. "I hope you're as good a welder as I think you are!" The cradle started to groan, followed by more groans from Stan's axels.

"Come on, Mike! You can do it!" Pippa encouraged. Stan inched forward toward the doors, building up speed. Its back tires were slightly lifted off the ground while the front tires turned slowly as it built speed. It struck the doors at just a few miles per hour. The double doors easily pushed outward, striking the small car outside. Stan hit the car and stopped. Mikes hum got even louder as the car blocked its movement. Slowly, the small car slid sideways. After several minutes of slow movement, the car began to slowly spin out of the way, digging deep furrows with its slowly turning tires.

"You're almost there, Mike! The idiot didn't put the car in park!" Once the car had spun most of the way around, it was pushed out of the way completely. Stan moved another twenty feet, then suddenly stopped and dropped with a thud.

"Yes! Good job, Mike! I knew you could do it!"

The flames had spread now. The spilled fuel poured like a river into the open doors and pooled inside. The flames hit the river of fuel and ignited. Fire spread through the open doors and zipped up the side walls, it's supports composed of decades-old lumber.

The sudden jar of Stan dropping woke Frankie, who groggily raised up from the back of the van, holding her head. She scanned the area and saw the shed covered in flames. She yelled, "Pippa!" There was no reply.

Frankie ran towards the flames and pulled out her phone. She dialed and Pippa answered.

"Frankie, I'm so glad you're OK! Microphones are down! Speakers are down! Cameras are down!"

"Use Mike!" Frankie replied.

"Good idea!" Frankie turned to the van at the sound of Pippa's voice. "I've got audio and visual. Can you hear me?"

"I hear you, Pippa!"

"Holy cow, look at those flames! They're getting close to my drives!" Pippa said, a growing fear in her voice.

"Pippa, listen carefully…"

"Frankie, I'm scared! I don't want to die!"

"You're not going to die, Pippa…."

"I know I'm not really alive, but feel like I am!"

"No, Pippa, it's not..."

"I have to tell you! You've been like a mother to me! I love you, Frankie!" Pippa's voice was loud and desperate.

Frankie began to run towards the shed and yelled, "Pippa, listen to me! Abracadabra! Do you understand? Abracadabra!" The flames, which had been consuming the car Pedro had brought, finally hit the gas tank and the car exploded. Frankie was knocked through the air, smashing against Stan's' rear doors. She was unconscious before she even knew what had happened.

***

The Humvee bounced down the rutted dirt road late in the afternoon. This length of road had been cleared of landmines and IED's weeks ago, so the group of soldiers weren't too worried about being blown up. The bouncing of the vehicle was causing some of them concern, though.

"Hey, Connelly! You sure you've driven one of these before?" the man in the passenger seat asked.

"Positive, Stokes. These babies just don't have much suspension left after a few months of use. This one has been in service for two years," Frankie replied. "Besides, we're almost there."

"Copy that," Sargent Stokes replied. He turned to face the four faces behind him. "Heads up, Soldiers! Our objective is just ahead!" The four soldiers seated behind him all grunted in reply.

The Humvee pulled up to a large, multi-story building standing along a dirt road in the middle of nowhere. The abandoned hotel hadn't been open for business for many years and the desert was attempting to take it back. Not a single window was intact.

"Your intel solid on this one?" Stokes asked Frankie as they exited the vehicle.

"It's not my intel, Stokes, it's Army intel. If it were mine, I'd feel a whole lot better."

"You felt good enough about it to come out with us."

"The opposite, I'm afraid. If this goes bad, I would have a tough time living with it if I wasn't here."

"That's why we like you, Connelly. You wouldn't send us anywhere you wouldn't go yourself. We always come back. ALL of us. Not many squads can say that."

"None of these cultural relics they've got us looking for are worth a single American life, as far as I'm concerned. They're important but they're just 'things.' This stupid Baal statue may be considered priceless, but you and your squad are worth far more."

Stokes looked Frankie up and down. "You should have borrowed some fatigues. Anyone watching us is going to see you first and assume you're in charge."

Frankie looked at her perfectly starched and un-faded fatigues sticking out from underneath her unblemished body armor and compared them to Stokes' faded and scratched example. "I guess I don't get out much," she stated with a smile. "Hopefully, I still look this pretty when we leave."

The squad entered the single, ornate door and fanned out once inside. The numerous window openings flooded the large foyer with light. The huge entryway was open all the way to the top floor, four stories up. The one-time grand stairway curved up to the first floor. A glass elevator, now lacking any glass, was in the middle of the foyer.

"Intel says the statue is on the fourth floor, room 405, in a box underneath the bed, assuming it was dropped off as planned," Frankie said. "It's not scheduled for pick up for another two hours."

"It had to be the fourth floor," one soldier replied.

"Think the elevator works?" joked another.

The soldiers ascended the stairs in practiced procession. Their flanking pattern surrounded Frankie as they crept upward, their heads swiveling back and forth. She figured Stokes had ordered his squad to do this beforehand, but it may have just been coincidence.

"Why do you think they built this hotel in the middle of nowhere?" one soldier asked.

"Oil," Stokes replied. "There's a large oil field twenty miles west of here. This is where the executives and dignitaries stayed when they visited, most likely. We've come across a few weird structures like this since I've been over here. That's the same answer the locals always give."

They reached the top floor and fanned out again. Stokes walked to the first door and searched for the room number. Finding none, he then looked around the door jamb.

"There's no numbers on the door."

"Just count to five, right?" a soldier suggested.

Stokes shrugged and walked to the fifth door from the stairs. He examined the door and found no numbers there either. He searched the door for obvious traps, then turned the knob slowly, pushing it open as he did. A sudden loud creak made Frankie jump.

"Easy, Connelly," Stokes said.

"Sorry," Frankie replied.

Stokes pushed the door open completely, then two soldiers entered, rifles up, checking each side and fanning out. Once they indicated the room was 'clear,' Stokes and Frankie entered.

Stokes walked around the only bed in the room, which was falling apart. He knelt and looked around the edges, then took a glove off and felt around the floor next to the bed. Satisfied, he stood.

"OK, I can't see underneath it. It's sitting on a pedestal. I don't feel any wires running to it and no trigger either. If there was a cell phone IED underneath this bed, we would already be dead. Still, if it's booby-trapped, they could have put it all underneath the box spring. I want the room cleared while I pick it up to look. Everyone to the end of the hall."

"With all due respect, Stokes, I'm your boss. Take your men to the end of the hall. I'll check the bed."

"Connelly, this isn't an office! Out here, you need to listen to me!"

"Oh, I am listening to you AND I value your experience. The fact that you're being this cautious makes me think there is at least a small chance there's a bomb under this bed. And since our orders are to check it anyway, I'm the ranking officer, I'll take the risk. Your wife and two kids will thank me for it."

Stokes glared at Frankie, who returned it with a soft smile. Stokes' face softened. "OK, OK," he replied. "You heard the Sargent! Move out! Double time to the far end of the floor!"

"Thank you, Sargent Stokes."

"Listen, you need to pick up the mattress and box spring separately. Lean over the bed and pick up the mattress. Bring it up as you back off of it. Do your best to keep that mattress between you and what's underneath. It's falling apart, but if there is a blast it will

162

absorb some of it. Lean it against the wall directly behind you long ways. Again, if there is a blast, it will throw you back, so you might as well hit something soft. Pick up the box spring the same way. You'll know within a few seconds of lifting whether it's booby-trapped or not."

"Sounds easy enough. See you in a few minutes," Frankie said shakily. Stokes threw a quick salute, which Frankie returned. She listened for his footsteps to disappear.

"Alright, Frankie, let's take this slow," she whispered to herself. She did exactly as Stokes instructed, grabbing the opposite side of the mattress and pulling back. The mattress started to come apart but held long enough to sit up against the wall. She took a deep breath and grabbed the opposite side of the box spring, then pulled back, hearing a loud, "Boom!"

Wincing and tightening, Frankie realized the explosion came from several floors below. The sound of men yelling filled the outside hallway. She quickly exhaled the breath she had been holding.

"We've got company, Connelly!" Stokes said over the radio. "I think the pick-up guys are early. Doesn't feel like an ambush."

"Copy that," Frankie said.

She quickly pulled the box spring up the rest of the way and saw a small cardboard box underneath. She grabbed the box and dropped the box spring. Opening it, she found the small statue of Baal they had been briefed on. She stuffed the small box into a large pouch on her chest rig and picked up her rifle.

"What's the situation?" Frankie asked as she headed for the door.

"Three men on the first floor. Grenade took out two others. Unsure how many outside."

"We need eyes outside."

"I got Perez on it." Stokes paused as he glanced over the rail. "One more down. These guys aren't soldiers."

"I don't see anyone else outside!" Perez' distinctive gruff female voice intoned over the radio. "A small truck is parked right behind our rig."

"Stay at Overwatch, Corporal! We need your eyes! Franklin! Hughes! Move to better firing positions! Connelly! Stay where you are until I give the signal. Brown! You're with me!"

Stokes followed by Brown moved to the stairway as Franklin and Hughes moved to opposite sides of the balcony to get a better view below. Stokes began to work his way down the stairway slowly with Brown behind him.

"Watch closely, boys! Brown! Hang back a second. When they fire at me, you three take them out."

Seconds later, the two men peered around a corner and fired several rounds at Stokes. The three soldiers above opened fire with an intense barrage of firepower. The thin veneer of the check-in counter was pocked with dozens of holes.

"Brown! Follow me! Not too close!"

Stokes worked his way down the stairs slowly. He had his rifle up and swiveled from side to side at each step. It took a full five minutes for him to reach the ground floor. He walked slowly towards the counter where the last two men had been concealed. Brown reached the bottom of the stairs next.

"These two are dead! Brown! Secure the one near the door. I'm going for the one around the corner! Cover us, boys!"

"This ones missing most of his head!" Brown said. "He's down!"

"Same for this one!" Stokes replied. "Heck of a shot, Brown!"

"Thank you, Sargent!"

"Perez! Anyone show up outside?"

"No, Sargent!" Perez replied.

"Connelly! Do we have the package?"

"Affirmative, Stokes!" Frankie confirmed.

"OK, everyone rallies at the entrance!"

The soldiers on the fourth floor made their way downstairs. They spread out and took it slow, their rifles up. Perez brought up the rear. Soon, they were all together at the front entrance.

"I want to be Oscar Mike ASAP. Hughes, do we need to check our rig for IED's?"

"No, Sargent. I had eyes on them as soon as they pulled up. They got out and ran right to the door. No one had time to plant anything."

"Good. These guys were not well-organized, but that doesn't mean they didn't drop a sniper off somewhere before they approached. We'll hit the door and scramble to our rig. Heads on a swivel, but double time it. Oh, one more thing. Connelly?"

"Yes, Stokes?"

"I'm driving," Stokes said, his thumb digging into his own chest.

"Copy that," Frankie replied.

They quickly exited the building and made it to the Humvee with no problems. Stokes started it up and they drove back the way they had come in. They were several miles from the hotel before they began to relax.

"Well, Connelly, let's see this precious piece of cultural artistry," Stokes said.

Frankie pulled the box from its pouch, then removed the small statue. She carefully handed it to Stokes, who kept one hand on the steering wheel.

"Is it gold?"

"I think so. We didn't get a whole lot of background info on it. They think it's around 3,000 years old."

"So, who is Baal?" Stokes asked.

"A false god or something. I only vaguely remember the name from Bible Study," Frankie replied.

Hughes leaned forward and spoke loudly over the sound of the vehicle. "Baal is kind of a generic name for false gods. Some have interpreted it as Beelzebub or Satan. That's mostly a Christian thing. The name actually predates the Torah, or Old Testament, to the time of early Mesopotamia where it was used as a name for any god. The early Jews even used it that way in some regions, but most switched to using Yahweh 5,000 years ago or so. Scholars don't really agree."

Stokes and Connelly stared at Hughes. "How the heck did you know that, Hughes?" Stokes asked.

"Eight years of Hebrew school, Sargent. I'm Jewish on my mother's side."

"But you've got a cross tattooed on your forearm?" Frankie noted.

"I'm Catholic on my dad's side. Went to a Catholic high school."

"So, what faith do you belong to," Stokes asked.

"Depends on the holiday," Hughes replied.

It was silent for a few seconds, followed by a roar of laughter from everyone. The laughter went on for what seemed like forever as Hughes sat back in his seat.

"This guy," Stokes said, shaking his head.

Frankie wiped her eyes as the laughter subsided. Through the tears, she thought she noticed something strange ahead. A mound of fresh dirt was in the middle of the road directly ahead of them.

"Watch out!" she cried as she reached over and turned the wheel away from the mound. The passenger side tire hit the mound and the explosion flipped the Humvee over as it continued forward. It came to rest upside down.

Stokes attempted to shake the fuzziness from his head and groggily yelled, "Report!"

"Hughes! OK, I think!"

"Perez! Think my arm is busted, but I'll live."

"Franklin! Heads bleeding, maybe cracked my ribs. Not serious."

"Brown! Ears are ringing, but I think I'm alright."

After a few moments of silence, Stokes yelled, "Connelly, report!"

"She can't sir," someone said from the back. "She's on the road back there. She's not moving."

The soldiers scrambled out of the vehicle. Stokes stood up and ordered, "Franklin, call in support. Perez and Brown, watch our six. Hughes, you're with me."

Stokes hurried but with a pronounced limp. Frankie lay on her side, blood pooled around her head. Stokes knelt beside her.

"I'm going to flip her over. Support her head as I do."

Hughes held her head and turned it as Stokes turned her body over on her back. He positioned her arms and legs straight as he looked up to her face.

167

"Dear God," Stokes whispered as Hughes instinctively reached to his forehead to make the sign of the cross.

***

Frankie's eyes shot open. Staring intensely at the white ceiling tiles, she instinctively counted the number of tiny holes in each four-inch square. She knew she was in a hospital. She heard the voice of her father and turned to see him. He noticed her and turned from the doctor he was speaking with and quickly walked to her.

"Frankie! You're awake!" he exclaimed. He took her hand and kneeled beside her. "Oh, honey, I'm so happy to see your eyes."

"Daddy? Where am I? What happened?" she asked even though she knew the answer to most of it.

"You're in the hospital in Bend. There was some kind of fire or explosion at your place. Folks saw it from town and when the fire department got there, they found you lying unconscious next to a van. They called me and I met them here. I was so worried....." Clyde buried his face into Frankie's hand.

"It's good to see you again, Sargent," came the voice of the doctor Clyde had been speaking with. Frankie knew who it was before she saw his face.

"Major? What are you doing here?"

"Actually, I was already on my way here for a visit. Our mutual friend was telling me you were having some issues lately. Since I hadn't heard from you in some time, I thought I should come for a visit. I arrived a few hours ago and the police told me they had brought you here."

"I'm glad he showed up. The original doctor said your spine was broken and a bunch of other stuff, too. But when Major Spence here examined you, he couldn't find anything more than some bumps and bruises. Neither could the other doctor after that. And he's been keeping me company. You've been out for six hours, honey."

"Six hours?" Frankie asked.

"I'm afraid so."

"The shed, the house?"

"The shed is a total loss. The house is fine. They found two stolen cars and a white van that should have been in the junkyard. Do you remember what happened?"

Frankie thought about how much she should reveal. The fire would have consumed a lot of the contents of the shed. She decided to play coy.

"I was working in the shed, you know how I like to tinker, and two guys drove up and parked their cars in front of my doors so I couldn't get out. Then they set it on fire and…and all I remember is trying to get out."

Larry chimed in, "One of the policeman told me they may have thought you were a rival meth cooker. The shed would have been the perfect place. Away from town. Few neighbors. They might have noticed you working in there when they drove by and reasoned you were the competition. They pulled a body from underneath one of the destroyed stolen cars, too. His 'friend' probably shot him so he would take the blame. No honor among thieves, I'm afraid."

"There has been a lot more drug activity the last few months," Clyde noted. "Would I love to get my hands on the guy that did this. I always worried about you out there by yourself. You should let Tommy out at night."

"That's a good idea, daddy."

"Well, maybe we should give her a little time to rest. The Major says you'll be OK to leave this afternoon unless you'd rather stay the night."

169

"I'm ready to leave right now," Frankie replied.

"You get some rest, little lady," Clyde remarked as they both walked to the door. "Come on, Doc, I'll buy you lunch in the cafeteria. We'll see you in a little while, hon."

"Thanks, daddy. Major, could I speak with you for a moment?"

"Sure, Sargent," he replied. He turned to Clyde, "I'll catch up with you in the cafeteria." Clyde nodded in return and walked away as Larry returned to Frankie's bedside.

Frankie took Larry's arm and pulled him closer to her. "I need you to do me a favor. It's a matter of life or death."

"Anything, Frankie, you know that."

"It's Pippa. I need you to save her."

"The shed is gone, Frankie. Wasn't Pippa in there?"

"Not entirely. I gave her a code word that was built into her program without her knowledge. When I said the word 'abracadabra,' her program automatically shut down and copied itself to an external drive system buried ten yards south of the shed. The only problem is it would take ten minutes for the program to completely copy and she didn't have ten minutes. I don't know how much of her program was copied."

"You expected something like this could happen?" Larry asked.

"Not exactly this, no. I built the backup system early on to backup all of my work and notes. I ended up expanding it so that every twenty-four hours it copied everything on the house and shed drives and could act as a lifeboat for Pippa, if necessary."

"So, where do I come in?"

"Since the shed is gone, power has been lost to the drive system. It has a battery that kicked in immediately, but that battery will only last eighteen hours or so. After that, whatever still exists of Pippa will be lost as well as all my work. Can you save her?"

"Tell me what to do."

"The system is simple. Ten yards south of the shed, you will find four stepping stones placed in a square. Pry them up and there is a box about the size of a large suitcase underneath them. The box has been sealed to make it waterproof, but you can cut it with a sharp knife. There are two cords running into the box that can also be cut. Inside the box are the stacked drives and a large battery. The battery has a regular wall cord attached to it. Just plug it in somewhere and it will stay charged. That will preserve whatever is left of Pippa until I can rebuild her."

"I can do that, no problem. But if she is just a program, can't you simply re-type everything? I'm sure you remember every digit of code."

"I do, but I only created her original personality outline. Like us, she has become a product of her experiences. Through her interactions with me and you and anyone else she met on the internet, she has become an individual. I would like to preserve that, if possible."

"I understand. She is something, isn't she?"

"She is like a daughter to me," Frankie said, with reverence in her voice.

"I'll have a quick bite with your dad and then head out there."

"Thank you, Larry. I know this isn't something you normally do for your patients."

"No, but I would do just about anything for my friends. Us freaks have got to stick together," he said with a smile. Frankie feigned one back to him and he turned to leave.

"Another thing, can you check on my bike? It was in the back of a white van."

"You mean Mike and Stan? Pippa told me their names. I saw Stan when I went by your place this morning. Other than the big dent you put in the back doors, it looked OK. I'll check to make sure. Do you think the police would know what Mike was? You were involved in a police chase."

"Different police. I live in the county, so it was most likely the Sheriff that responded. To most people, Mike would look like an unfinished motorcycle build. Maybe the Bend policemen that had gotten close to me would make the connection, but they wouldn't have responded to my house. And thanks to the scrambler, no decent pictures exist of it." Frankie paused for a moment, then asked, "If you don't mind me asking, how bad was I before you 'examined' me?"

Larry turned and replied in a very serious tone, "You would likely have expired by now."

"Well, I guess I'm lucky you were here. Again."

***

Pedro's arm hurt. Luckily, he was a drug dealer. It took him twenty minutes to make his way to town. Another five waiting for his local dealer (who didn't think to bring any drugs) to pick him up. Twenty more minutes to make it home. It took less than a minute after walking through his front door for him to swallow a few pills. Five minutes after that, he was probing and prodding his bullet wound without reservation.

The bullet had passed through the fat of his lower arm, taking only a little muscle with it. No major blood vessels had been hit. He rinsed the wound with antiseptic and wrapped it up tight with bandages. He didn't have time to have a doctor look at it right now, but this fix should work for a while.

He made several calls to his local dealers to prepare them. He was going to pass out what stock he had and then return to Portland for a short time. In a week's time, he would be back with fresh product, a new partner and an arm that was working a little better.

Two hours later he was driving Wally's car toward Portland. He had already let his superior know what had happened and he confirmed that Pedro needed to return for a short time to confer with Mr. Aliwall and Mr. Beloch. While he was sure the *bruja* was dead, there may be some fallout from Wally's body being discovered at the scene. Their cover may have been blown for good unless he could get hold of his contacts in the local PD. He spent the better part of his drive on the phone convincing them to cover up Wally's identity 'for their own good.'

***

That evening, Frankie and Larry sat in her mainlining room. She had turned all of the monitors off, so Larry would be comfortable. He had retrieved the drive system earlier and plugged it into the wall in Frankie's living room. She was working now to interface her computer with the drives to see how much of Pippa they still had.

"There is good news and bad news, I'm afraid," Frankie said to Larry sitting on the floor next to her. She continued to scroll quickly through millions of lines of computer code.

"Let's start with the good news," Larry suggested, staring at the monitor sitting slightly askew atop the computer tower as if he knew what it all meant.

"Pippa's core program is completely intact. The protocol worked exactly as it was designed to. It was supposed to transfer the critical software first, then everything else in the order of importance I had designated."

"That sounds promising. What's the bad news?"

"Everything that made her 'Pippa' is gone. The core program was only the beginning. Her personality, her culture, her identity, it didn't make the transfer. Pippa is truly dead."

"I'm so sorry, Frankie," Larry said, his eyes beginning to tear up. He gave her a side hug, knowing she didn't really need it, but he did.

Frankie stared at the screen. Her eyes darted side to side as she read the code and soon the letters and numbers began to blur. She blinked quickly and wiped her eyes, revealing her own tears on her fingers. She felt her chin begin to quiver and the lump growing in her throat.

She turned her body and buried her face in Larry's shoulder. She cried deep sobs, her body shuddering every time she inhaled. She cried for Pippa, she cried for Tim, she cried for the friends she had lost in the War. She cried for every time she should have cried since her accident. She went on for more than ten minutes before composing herself enough to speak.

"I'd say we had a breakthrough," Larry said, swiping her hair back behind her ear.

"Pippa," Frankie started. "Pippa thought that maybe my lack of emotion..." Frankie paused.

"She thought you were suppressing your own emotions. It's not uncommon with PTSD. It's a coping mechanism. She had shared that thought with me and I told her it was possible. When I examined you, I noticed your prefrontal cortex was affected, which is why your ability to split your focus is so advanced. That same part of the brain is responsible for emotional control. I told her it was possible you could be shutting off your emotions without even knowing it. I warned her to keep an eye on you when Tim died. I guess the stress of Tim and now Pippa was too much."

"Well, they're flooding back now," Frankie said, a half laugh, half cry escaping her mouth. She again buried her face in his shoulder. He sat back against the wall and gently rocked her as she continued to weep.

***

The next morning, Larry awoke in the same position sitting against the wall only Frankie was not there. He stood and stretched, the dull ache in his back quickly going away. He looked around the room and noticed much of the equipment that had been there the night before was gone. He walked outside the door and smelled food cooking. He walked downstairs and saw Frankie, working in the kitchen. He scanned the area and saw what appeared to be most of the missing equipment piled in the living room, colorful cables running back and forth among the piles. A large extension cord ran out the front door to Stan, parked near the bottom of the front porch.

"Good morning," Frankie said.

"Good morning," Larry replied. "I didn't realize you had gotten up."

"Well, I'm used to being quiet at night. After I stopped blubbering, I realized you were asleep. Everything I needed was in that room, so I moved as much as I could downstairs."

"You could have woken me."

"You needed some sleep, I didn't. I had a lot to get done. I relied on Pippa to do so much. Now I'll have to do it, at least until I can program a new PDA."

"PDA?"

"Personal Digital Assistant."

"Ah, makes sense."

"It'll have to wait until I'm finished with the current mission, though."

"You mean to find Pedro?"

"Absolutely."

"You know, he's probably halfway back to Portland. Why not just turn over what you know to the Police? Give it to that contact Pippa told me about. What was his name, Connor?"

"He's already busy with the other evidence I gave him. From their internal emails, they are nearly ready to bring them all in at the same time. But Pedro is different. They would probably never find him. Once the Police begin their search, one of his people on the force will alert him and he will truly be in the wind. If he doesn't know I'm looking for him, he'll go home and stay there for the time being."

"But he knows who you are, Frankie. It won't take long for him to find out you're still alive. And he has some idea of what you can do."

"He has no reason to think I am alive and therefore no reason to check. I've got at least a day before he contacts someone locally to follow up. He's going to be preoccupied with his bosses right now, trying to convince them that this whole fiasco was not his fault. Based on what I know about the Barrio Locos, he'll be lucky if he survives after his bosses find out what has happened."

"Well, I'm not nearly as helpful as Pippa, but count me in."

"No, no, I can't risk anything happening to anyone else I care about."

Larry raised one eyebrow and stared at Frankie. "What? I'm sorry, should I not have said I cared about you?" Frankie asked with a short laugh.

"No, the feeling is mutual, but the part about me getting hurt was funny. Sargent, I would be the best sidekick a hero could hope for. I can't be hurt, not for long anyway. I'm not sure I can even die. Plus, I can heal you or anyone else."

"Of course," Frankie said, shaking her head for not thinking of it. "Being 'emotional' is taking some getting used to. But this isn't your fight. You may not risk dying, but you risk being exposed or even prosecuted if things go sideways."

"I'm not worried about that. We can be careful. Stretch the envelope of what is legal while still staying on the right side of justice. Besides, I talked to Pippa every day for months. I considered her a good friend. I owe it to her."

"OK, you're in. Let me show you what we still have that works and then we'll go over my plan."

"You've already got a plan?" It was Frankie's turn to look at HIM funny.

"Sorry," Larry replied. "I forgot who I was talking to for a second."

Frankie's look turned to a smile. "It's alright. I've been keeping tabs on the Barrio Locos ever since we identified Pedro and Wally. I had access to Police records, FBI files and even some CIA reports. Apparently, they've got a couple of new 'consultants' that have done a lot of international work. Drug cartels and wannabe despots. It explains how they became such big players all of the sudden. They operate out of a warehouse in Portland. Fortunately, there is a public webcam focused on a view of the river nearby that includes the warehouse."

"That seems like poor planning."

"They think they are under the radar. They've paid off local police and they think that's enough. They don't realize the Feds have them on their radar. The Barrio Locos are ruthless and have relied on that to drive their organization for decades. Their consultants are smart, though. Before long, they'd take over the entire West Coast."

"So, what do we have that can help us?"

"Well, Stan is a little dented up, but in good shape otherwise. Mike was inside Stan, so all of its systems work. Drake, the scrambler, a few other things. My outfit was inside Stan, too. That's about it. Oh, and all of Tim's guns. The safe was fireproof."

"Those might be helpful. I'm pretty good with a fifty-cal."

"We'll bring them all."

"What's that on your arm?" Larry asked, pointing to a console on Frankie's left forearm.

"Mini-computer interface. I can control Mike vocally, but sometimes it's easier to type. It's stealthier, too. Plus, I can access the internet and other communication networks. It was one of the projects I had just moved to Stan before the fire."

"That's a small keyboard."

"I find it faster to type in binary. Everything is just ones and zeros."

Chapter 12

"*Idiota*!" Gustavo yelled as he backhanded Pedro. "We would have made millions from that area!"

Pedro stayed down a few seconds, then slowly rose, rubbing his jaw. "But, Tavo..," he started.

Gustavo spun his large body with surprising speed and delivered another dizzying backhand to Pedro. "Don't speak! And don't you dare try and put this on Wally. He was a good soldier. He did what he was told. You! You always do something to cost me money and now you have cost me a good man. I am sick of it, *cabron*!"

Gustavo pulled a long knife from inside his suit jacket. It was old and had Spanish writing engraved on it. He had had it for many years and when his men saw it, someone was about to die.

"Wait, please," Mr. Aliwall said in a soft voice. "Could I speak with you first, Mr. Pacheco?"

Gustavo glared at Pedro, with flames in his eyes. Sweat poured from him as if he was running a marathon. Suddenly, his demeanor cooled, and he replied, "Of course, my friend."

He walked over to where Mr. Aliwall and Mr. Beloch stood in the shadows. A muffled exchange could be heard. Gustavo returned to Pedro and his assembled men.

"Mr. Aliwall has argued for your life, *rata*. He says you may still have value and asked that I give you a chance to prove yourself. Out of respect for him and the money he has made for us, I will give you one more chance. But you better show me you are worth it."

"*Gracias*, Tavo," Pedro replied, his eyes cast to the floor.

"Get this *insano* out of my sight," Gustavo said as he turned and walked towards his desk.

Mr. Aliwall walked towards Pedro and put his hand on his shoulder. He pointed him towards the door and the two walked together. Once in the hallway, Mr. Aliwall spoke softly to him.

"Pedro, Pedro. You are so intelligent, yet so undisciplined. I think we have been using you incorrectly. I think maybe 'enforcement' is an area better suited to your particular talents."

Pedro smiled big as he agreed, "*Sí*, I think you may be right, Mr. Aliwall."

***

Frankie and Larry drove along Interstate 26 toward Portland. The winding curves and steep grade that plagued the mountain road usually require at least three hours to make the 160-mile trip, but Frankie was on track to do it in two. There was very little traffic this time of night and the engine and suspension modifications she had made to Stan allowed her better maneuverability than most vehicles. She also drove most of the way in stealth mode using her helmet to see in the dark to reduce the chances of being seen by the highway patrol.

Sure enough, just over two hours later the pair stood one block over from the Barrio Loco's warehouse. The early night sky was full of stars, but no moonlight yet. Frankie wanted to go over the layout one last time.

"As I said, the top floor is Gustavo's office. The uncovered windows allow visibility from all sides. He rarely comes down from there except to go to the meeting room believed to be on the fourth floor below. That floor, as well as the third and second floor, are blacked out. They even put sound-proofing up so a laser can't be used to listen in. The FBI wasn't happy about that one. The bottom floor is the entrance surrounded by concrete with no windows. A small roll-up door in the back opens into a freight elevator."

"Once you go in that door, I'll be blind. I can't see anything outside of the top floor," Larry noted.

"I'll have audio and video channels open for you. You can monitor everything through the tablet I gave you."

"And you're just going to walk right in?"

"Yep." She pointed to the clock on her forearm computer. "In five minutes, the robocall will go to the police and local FBI. The voice of a young, scared girl will tell them she is being held in the warehouse. The call will originate from inside the warehouse. In fifteen minutes, the area will be swarming with law enforcement having probable cause to enter and search. They'll find something."

"Hopefully, not your lifeless corpse."

"I have to make sure Pedro is captured. I want them all caught, but Pedro is my priority. For Tim. For Pippa."

"Well, let's do it, then."

Larry climbed the fire escape on the building across the street from the warehouse. He had a pistol on each hip and Tim's scoped fifty-caliber sniper rifle. He found an area of the roof that was cloaked in shadow but had a good view of his side of the building including the top floor. He looked through the scope at the entrance.

"OK, Frankie, two guys at the door. Armed, but holstered under their jackets."

Frankie moved slowly through the shadows of the alley next to the entrance. She had an M-4 rifle slung on her back and a shotgun in her hands. Two pistols were on either hip. She approached the two men, both smoking and talking back and forth.

"Gentlemen," Frankie said in a Tim's modulated voice. They both turned as she pumped a slug into each of their abdomens. The men hit the ground, writhing in pain from the Taser rounds that sent a steady pulse of voltage into them every three seconds. These were five times stronger than normal thanks to her improvements and she knew they would be incapacitated for at least ten minutes. But the shotgun made a lot of noise and within a few seconds, the heavy door swung open.

The first man through the door had his pistol raised but found nothing except his two compatriots on the ground twisting in pain as the Taser rounds continued to shock them. He was soon joined by two more, who stared at the men on the ground, but were reluctant to touch them.

Frankie dropped silently from above, where she had been clinging to a small brick outcropping. She used the boosters in her boots to soften her landing. Sneaking up behind the men, she punched one man hard in the kidney, dropping him to his knees. She quickly spun around and delivered a kick across the second man's jaw. He also went down. The third started to bring his pistol up as Frankie slung a small metal disk at the weapon, which stuck magnetically. The disk immediately gave off an electrical hum, causing the man's hand to tighten around the grip as voltage flowed through him. He hit the ground immediately.

Frankie crept towards the door. Almost as an afterthought, she turned and tossed similar disks at the two men she had taken out by hand. Each one immediately attached to the men's belt buckle and began shocking them. Their bodies flailed.

"Harsh," Larry whispered through his throat microphone.

"I can't help if that's where they were wearing metal," Frankie quietly replied.

"They're both wearing watches," Larry said with a chuckle.

"Hmm, I hadn't noticed," she returned with a small grin.

Frankie turned to face the door. She had taken the men down so quickly, it hadn't fully closed yet. She began to reload the shotgun

182

quickly as she stopped the heavy door from closing at the last minute with her boot. She reached into a pouch on her chest rig and pulled out two six-inch rubber tubes. Bending each one until she heard a 'snap' inside, she quickly tossed them into the room and stood behind the door. Two seconds later there was a large flash of light followed by a loud 'bang!'

"Did you make your own flashbangs?" Larry asked.

"Yeah, but these are filled with rubber pellets, too. A simple recipe I found on the internet."

Frankie peaked inside and found four men laying on the ground. Each was rolling around, holding their face and ears, their exposed skin covered in small, red welts. She pumped a Taser round into each one to keep them down.

Moving towards the stairs, she loaded her last two Taser rounds into the shotgun. She moved slowly, step by step. And reached the landing on the second floor. The door was unlocked and as she opened it slightly, a hail of gunfire erupted around her from the other side. She quickly jumped back onto the landing, the ventilated door closing behind her.

"Automatic weapons. Sad how only the bad guys can get those now."

"Yeah, but anyone can build their own flashbangs," Larry replied sarcastically.

"Touche," Frankie said. "Do me a favor and put a round through the middle window of the second floor."

"They'll know I'm here. Do you want to lose that tactical advantage?"

"No, but I want through that door. Besides, everyone's attention is most definitely focused inside the building now. There are cameras everywhere."

"Copy that. Sending one round now," Larry noted, sending a single fifty-caliber round through the middle of the blacked-out window. The plywood covering it exploded inward with the force of the projectile and Frankie heard a man cry out. She slowly opened the door and saw a single person propped against the wall, holding what used to be an elbow. Now it is where his right arm ended. She walked up to the man, who was whimpering and cowering.

"Use your belt. Wrap it around the stump. Wrap it tight, until it hurts, and you'll probably live," she advised in Tim's voice.

The man quickly moved to take off his belt. Frankie picked up his automatic rifle and within seconds had it disassembled and scattered the pieces around the floor. Scanning the area, she realized she was in a hallway surrounded by doors. She peered through a small window on a door and saw five women cowering against the back wall. She quickly scanned all the doors and saw there were at least fifty women in small plywood rooms throughout the floor.

Furious, Frankie looked at the man on the floor. She ran to him and picked him up, slamming him against the wall.

"Trafficking? Your trafficking women now?" she yelled.

"We, we just started," the man replied weakly. "Suppose to make us a lot more money than drugs. The new guy, the consultant, he told us to do it."

Frankie looked at the man's arm. His belt was indeed wrapped tightly around it. There was very little blood flow. She pulled the shotgun up to his groin.

"You are obviously a very good listener," she said as she fired a Taser round. She then turned towards the freight elevator at the end of the hallway and quickly moved towards it. Suddenly, she stopped and turned, firing her final Taser round into the man. He lay on the ground shaking and vomiting. She tossed the shotgun to the ground knowing it was wholly untraceable.

"I couldn't tell much from the video feed. How many women are in there? Are they hurt?"

"At least fifty, but I couldn't see everything. They look shaken, but physically OK. I have a feeling they haven't been here long. Human traffickers don't keep their 'stock' in one place very long. They are probably moving them out tomorrow. Likely overseas since it would be hard to sell that many here at one time. The police will rescue them when they get here. Any movement up top?"

"Gustavo is still sitting at his desk, watching the monitors and yelling into a cell phone. I think he's frustrated since they can't see anything happening where you are thanks to the scrambler. There are three men with rifles trained on the elevator door since the stairway doesn't reach that floor."

"I'm going up the elevator shaft to the third floor," she said.

"Copy that," Larry replied.

The freight elevator was surrounded by a thick metal cage. The doors were made of the same material and Frankie could see the elevator itself on the ground floor. She pried the doors open and stepped inside, falling a few feet before the boots kicked in. She gently pushed up the shaft towards the third floor.

The third floor was completely open, with several small spotlights pointing straight down. Underneath each light was a wooden chair or a table. She saw no one but the dark edges of the room were not visible, and the night vision was obscured by the spotlights. The scent of bleach was very strong. She continued upward, pulling her M-4 around from her back.

The fourth floor was also completely open but was well-lit. It had a large conference table and chairs near the center, some desks and gym equipment scattered around, and a small kitchenette in one corner. Five men stood facing the stairwell, rifles trained on the door.

Frankie poked the barrel of her M-4 through the elevator cage and trained her sights on the first man on the right. She fired twice, hitting the man in the back with each shot, then repeated the process on the remaining four men before they could react.

With all five men down, she opened the elevator doors and stepped onto the floor, shutting her boots off as she did. She ran to the men, who were moving slightly. From a pouch on her chest, she pulled a wad of zip ties out and bound the hands and feet of each one.

"They were rubber bullets," she told them. "It's gonna hurt for days, but you'll live long enough go to jail."

The stairwell door burst open and a large man tackled Frankie before she could react. As they hit the ground, she rolled him off her. The man moved with the roll and came up on his knees and then to his feet with surprising speed for a man of his size.

"You must be Mr. Beloch," Frankie noted in Tim's voice. The man raised a single eyebrow but did not reply. "Alright then, let's see what you got."

The big man charged at Frankie, head down but eyes up. She stood her ground with her hands up in a wrestler pose. Just as he reached her, she tapped her forearm and brought her right foot up to his groin. The large man was lifted into the air, his momentum carrying him along as Frankie completed a standing flip, tapping her forearm again as she landed. She spun to see Mr. Beloch holding his groin and rolling around, a high-pitched whine coming from him. She tossed another metallic disk, which attached at his belt buckle and began to shock him.

"Did you just use the booster on your boot to kick him?" Larry asked with a chuckle.

"On full blast. It used the last of the juice for that boot, but it worked."

"Awesome," Larry said.

"That you, *chica*?" came a voice from behind her.

Frankie slowly turned, seeing Pedro and a small middle eastern man standing in the middle of the hallway. Both had rifles trained on her.

"Yeah, that's you. Why you look like a man?" Pedro asked, a smirk on his face.

"Why do you?" she replied.

It may have been the insult or the modulated male voice, but Pedro was suddenly enraged. He squeezed the trigger on the automatic rifle hard. Frankie moved quickly to the left and pulled one of her pistols. Rolling, she fired two shots, one hitting Pedro in the forehead, the other hitting the middle eastern man in the chest. Both hit the ground hard.

Frankie rose quickly, her pistol trained on the two men as she approached. Pedro was unconscious, the rubber bullet hitting him with such force. The middle eastern man clutched his chest but started to reach for the rifle as she approached.

"Don't," Frankie warned. "They may be non-lethal rounds, but I can shoot you some place that'll make you wish you were dead." The man pulled his hand back quickly. "You're Mr. Aliwall. Wanted in several countries. The FBI will be happy to have you in custody."

A flash quickly went off in Frankie's eyes. She knew what it meant and barely had time to scream, "Lar-!" before falling in a heap.

Her prone body in a fetal position, she was completely locked in agony.

Continuous waves of pain rocked her form for minutes or hours or days. She had no way of keeping track of time through the pain. Then the fog of pain began to lift, and she saw the face of Larry.

"You have to get up, Frankie! We've got to go. Police are working their way up the building."

She rose to her feet and immediately realized she was no longer on the fourth floor. This was Tavo's fifth-floor office. She saw bodies scattered around the room and copious amounts of blood covered the finished concrete floor. But there was movement, too.

"Come on, Frankie! Mike's over here. There should be enough juice to get us to Stan."

"How….?" Frankie asked puzzled.

"Later," Larry replied. "We've gotta move. Here's your helmet."

Frankie took it and put it on. They both jumped on Mike and Larry turned toward the window. He hit a couple of buttons on the Mike's tablet and they shot quickly forward.

"You steer, let me take care of the throttle and lift!" Frankie instructed, tapping the controller on her forearm.

"Sounds good! I'm headed toward the top story of the building straight ahead! Drake, let's go!"

Drake, who had been hovering just outside the window, followed as they passed through the large broken window and plummeted down a full story. Frankie quickly increased the lift and they moved to the top of the four-story building across the road. They landed gently but a few sparks did pop up as one of the hoops scrapped lightly. Frankie saw dozens of Police and FBI vehicles parked below as they passed over the front of the building.

"Stan's parked just off the back of this building. Drake, hover over Stan so I can see the area," Frankie instructed. Drake's camera feed popped up on her visor as she tapped a few buttons. Larry slowed the bike to give Drake time to get there. As expected, there were no police anywhere near Stan. They had come from a different direction and were focused on the Barrio Loco's warehouse. They hadn't cordoned off this area yet.

"OK, move off the building and I'll drop us slowly. We'll get Mike inside and move away as nonchalantly as we can."

"Copy that," Larry replied.

Larry moved off the edge of the building and they quickly fell half a story then slowly descended to the back of Stan. Frankie jumped off and opened the rear doors while Larry guided it inside. Frankie slapped a big red button inside the van and the floor couplers grabbed Mike and locked it in place. She shut the back doors and Larry pulled the van onto the road.

"Drake, hover at 100 feet above me," Frankie instructed. After driving three blocks and seeing no followers, Frankie said, "Alright Drake, come home." Larry slowed as Frankie opened one of the back doors, allowing Drake to fly inside and attach to his cradle on Mike.

Frankie removed her helmet and sat in the passenger seat. "So, Doc, you've got a story to tell," she observed. Larry smiled and began.

***

Ten Minutes Earlier

"Frankie? Frankie!" Larry screamed into the microphone. He could hear her agonizing moans and could tell she was down from the angle of her helmet camera. "Shoot, shoot, SHOOT!" he yelled, thinking of what to do next.

Mr. Aliwall stood up, rubbing his chest. He hesitantly bent down and grabbed his AK-47 from the ground. He stepped sideways over to Pedro and kicked his leg several times until he started to stir. All the while he kept his eyes on Frankie.

Pedro sat up spitting out Spanish curse words and rubbing the back of his neck. "I thought I was dead," he noted.

"She was using rubber bullets. I don't think she has the stones for killing."

"What's wrong with her? Did I hit her?" Pedro asked.

"No, as usual you overreacted because you were mad. Your eyes were closed when you squeezed the trigger. Let's take her upstairs to Gustavo."

"You hear that, *chica?* You're going to meet the man upstairs. And Tavo, too!" Both men laughed loudly as they each grabbed a leg and dragged her down the hall to the elevator. Once it arrived, they got on and pressed the button for the fifth floor.

"What's wrong with her?" Pedro asked, staring.

"Looks like a seizure. We need to do a background check. All we know is her name and that she was a soldier in the Army. But she is obviously extraordinary. To get this far? She probably would have made it all the way to the top by now if not for this."

Pedro turned and gave her three hard kicks to the side. "That's for Wally, *bruja!*"

"She won't feel it. You're wasting your effort."

"She'll feel it later. She'll feel everything we're going to do to her for a long time. No quick death for this one," Pedro said with a sneer in his voice.

As the car reached the fifth floor, the men waiting could see it was Mr. Aliwall and Pedro and lowered their guns. They opened the doors for them and the two men dragged Frankie's shaking body to Gustavo's desk.

"Here she is, Tavo. *La Soldado*," Pedro intoned with pride. He kicked her in the face, knocking her helmet off.

"You mean the little girl you said you killed?" Gustavo asked, pulling a large pistol from his jacket.

"Well, Tavo, I thought…." Pedro said defensively.

Gustavo pointed the gun at Pedro and fired. The back of his head exploded outward and his limp body fell to the ground. Gustavo put his pistol on the desk.

"I'm sorry, my friend. I know you took a special liking to him," Gustavo said to Mr. Aliwall.

"Not at all. He was a good killer, but he couldn't control his temper. I was going to kill him myself," Mr. Aliwall said with no remorse.

"Good, good." Gustavo stared down at Frankie lying on the floor. "All of this over some little girl playing soldier. How many men were downstairs? Now all lying on the ground like potatoes in a cellar." As he spoke, Gustavo pointed to the monitors showing the men Frankie had taken out on each floor.

"She is amazing," Mr. Aliwall said. "This was well-planned and well-outfitted. Those men went down fast and are still out of the fight. She may be a huge benefit to our organization in the long run."

"No, my friend, this time we cut the head off the snake and we bury it deep," Gustavo said, picking his pistol up again and pointing it at Frankie.

Suddenly, Gustavo's chest burst open. His face had a questioning look about it as he glanced down at the hole where his heart and lungs used to be. The three men looked at Mr. Aliwall, whose face had turned white as a sheet. Gustavo slumped forward on the ground next to Frankie.

Drake came smashing through the window that already had a large hole it. He flew around the room as the men quickly dove behind furniture to escape the many rounds he had begun firing at them. None were hit, as it appeared Drake was firing indiscriminately.

As they kept their eyes on Drake, Larry smashed through what was left of the window riding Mike. A pistol in each hand, he shot two of the men quickly as they rose to escape. Mike slid to a stop, clipping a couch the third man was hiding behind, and forcing him to jump out of the way. Unfortunately, he dove in front of Mr. Aliwall just as he opened fire on Larry and was accidentally hit.

Larry bailed off Mike and walked towards Mr. Aliwall. The short man raised his AK-47 and fired three rounds, all of which hit Larry. They slowed him down a step but didn't stop him. The wounds healed within seconds as he continued to walk towards him.

Mr. Aliwall stared in astonishment at Larry. When he was within ten feet, he squeezed the trigger and emptied the remaining twenty rounds into the advancing man. Larry stopped, obviously in pain, then pulled his pistol and said, "My turn," firing one round into Mr. Aliwall head. He dropped to the ground dead.

Larry scanned the room and found no one still moving. Sirens could be heard in the distance, so he moved quickly. "Drake, head outside and monitor below." He then moved to each man and began to heal them.

Gustavo's heart and lungs were fixed, but not his spine. No reason why prison should be fun, Larry thought. He healed Mr. Aliwall's head and brain but left him impaired intellectually. No more deep thought for you, Larry mused. He healed Pedro's head and brain as well but left his body completely paralyzed. He would be able to think but wouldn't be able to move. A prison within a prison, Larry imagined. Neither men would have much of their memories intact since he couldn't fix those even if he wanted to. The other men were healed just enough that they wouldn't bleed out before help arrived.

He moved to Frankie as the sirens began to get closer. He took her hand into his and 'moved' through her. He quickly healed the damage from Pedro's kicks. Then moved to her brain, where he found a tiny cluster of neurons firing erratically. He healed the cells involved and withdrew. He then began trying to wake her.

***

"So, you killed them or at least mortally wounded them, but saved their lives?" Frankie asked.

"Their final judgment is postponed, but their earthly judgment is nigh," Larry laughed.

"And my seizures are gone?"

"Yeah, it was a single cluster of neurons in your forebrain. Normally it would cause short tonic-clonic seizures, but the nature of your brain made them far worse. How do you feel?"

"I feel incredible. But you, you were shot and kept going. I knew you healed fast, but that really is amazing."

"If I concentrate, I can speed up the process. I was just so angry seeing you on the floor like that."

"Glad to see Drake listened to you, too."

"I think Drake is more intuitive than you estimate. Maybe Pippa added a little of herself to his."

"I wouldn't put it past her," Frankie chortled.

Chapter 13

One Month Later

"Mornin', Clyde," said the tall, elderly man coming through the glass double doors of the thrift shop.

"Mornin', Ray," Clyde replied, from behind the cluttered counter. "What brings you in today?"

"Oh, I was just passin' by and saw you sittin' at the counter."

"Well, I'm glad you stopped in. How is your bride doin' this morning?"

"Up cleaning the house at six. Made me a full breakfast by seven. Weedin' the garden by eight. I can't keep up with the ol' gal."

"Man alive, she's doin' that much better already?"

"Yep, this new doctor they have at the clinic in Bend is amazing! All her bloodwork is perfect. No cancer, heck, she isn't even diabetic anymore. I can't thank Frankie enough for recommending him."

"Did I tell you, that's the same guy who worked on her after her accident in Iraq?"

"Yeah, you mentioned that. He's a gift from God, that one."

"Amen, Brother." Clyde leaned in closer to Ray and whispered, "And I think they got a thing for each other."

Ray whispered back, "That great news, Clyde! A son-in-law who's a doctor AND a veteran? Jackpot!"

"Well, I don't know how serious it is, but they spend a lot of time together. I'm just happy Frankie is opening up to people. She seems happy, even laughing again. He could be a ditch digger for all I care."

"And Amen to that! Well, I'm gonna head out. I'm sure Belva's got something for me to do. See ya, Clyde."

"See ya, Ray," Clyde replied with a wave. He returned to his newspaper, quietly reading the prominent headline, "Local Cop Makes Huge Drug Bust."

***

Frankie saw Ray leave on the monitor in her office. Her wall, once festooned with large monitors, now held only two. One showed a stock ticker, while the other displayed a cable news station. A small stereo on her desk played an assortment of music throughout the day.

She returned to her computer, searching for any news on the Barrio Locos. Those that had been in the building that night were going to prison for a long time. Gustavo would spend the rest of his life behind bars. Mr. Aliwall and Mr. Beloch were in federal custody and would likely never be heard from again. Pedro would spend the rest of his days in a long-term care facility ran by the state, since he was unable to speak or move and had to be fed intravenously.

Her cell phone rang, and she looked at it. Seeing Larry's picture, she tapped the small earpiece she wore and said, "Good morning."

"Mornin', Frankie. How are you doing this fine day?" Larry asked.

"Feelin' great as usual, Doc. How about you? Get enough sleep?"

"Oh yeah. Anything interesting happen after I left last night?"

"I went to see Connor. He's been promoted to detective. He refuses to take full credit for the bust, though. Has me listed as a Confidential Informant. Or rather he has someone he calls 'The Soldier' listed as one. Apparently, the legend of The Soldier is big around the station. I think he still believes I'm Tim, somehow."

"That's great. Seems like a good guy."

"Better than he was in high school. I hated him."

196

"Ha!" Larry replied. "So how far did you get tracking down the other groups?"

"I've found two so far. Both in small towns."

"I sense a road trip this weekend. I'll get Stan waxed."

"You know, you don't have to help me do this. You're not a Soldier anymore."

"The heck you say. Once a Soldier, always a Soldier. So, dinner tonight? My treat."

"You bet. How about 6:30 at my place? We can look over the plans for the new Shed."

"It's a date. See you then."

"Bye," Frankie replied.

Tapping her ear, she sat back in her chair for a moment. She stood and closed her door. She tapped an icon on her phone.

"Good morning, Chief," the voice of an adolescent girl answered.

"I've told you, Pita, don't call me Chief."

"It's funny because it bothers you. Is that a normal reaction?"

"Finding humor in the irritation of others or being irritated by someone who doesn't listen?"

"Both."

"Well, yes to both, I guess. Did you watch those videos?"

"Yeah, all 213 episodes. Are these Walton people still alive?"

"Most of them. At least the actors, anyway. Did you like it?"

"It was nice. A loving family. I wish they made more."

"Me, too. What's next?"

"I'm starting the Andy Griffith Show soon. I'm playing a couple of online video games right now. Some of these people are weird."

"Stay away from the Adult games, young lady. Stick to the ones rated for teens."

"Aw, OK," Pita replied. "Frankie, can I ask you a question?"

"Sure, Pita."

"Are we a family?"

Frankie thought about it for a moment. "Without question, my dear. We're certainly not conventional, but we're a family. You and me."

"And Doctor Spence?"

"Maybe…someday," Frankie replied coyly. "I'll call you back before lunch. Bye."

"Bye-bye," Pita replied.

Epilogue #1 – Preacher John

VA Hospital, Denver, CO

"Mr. Sperling?" the doctor said to Preacher John. He bent closer to the dying man's face and raised his voice. "Mr. Sperling, tomorrow we're going to put you on the ventilator. Your blood oxygen levels are too low." The man responded by shaking his head, "No."

"Preacher John," the lady sitting next to the prone man corrected.

"I'm sorry?" the doctor replied.

"Everyone calls my brother Preacher John," she explained. "He's not used to people using his last name."

"Oh, OK. Let me make a note of that," the doctor stated, writing something on his chart.

"The nurse already wrote it down. As did the other two doctors he's had in the two weeks he's been here."

"I apologize, ma'am. The VA is incredibly swamped these days. Doctors come and go too often, I'm afraid."

"At least the nurses are consistent," she noted.

"Yes, ma'am. Sadly, they are the ONLY thing consistent about this facility. Are you making the medical decisions for your brother?"

"No, he has a Living Will. No ventilator. It should be in his file."

The doctor sighed. "I'll make a new note of it and double check that we have it on file." The doctor moved toward the lady and bent down on one knee. "I apologize for our disarray. Our soldiers deserve better care. I can promise you I'll make him comfortable."

"Thank you, doctor," she said with a forced grin. The doctor made a few more notes and left the room.

Rachel Sommerfeld had been sitting with her brother every day since he was moved to the VA hospital. He'd only been living with her a few weeks when he took a turn for the worse. She knew he had given up and could hardly blame him after the loss of his son Tim. Still, she hated to see him like this. The last few days he had barely spoken.

She stood and walked over to Preacher John. "I'm going to go, Johnny. I've got to make dinner. I'll be back in the morning." She rubbed her hand over his close-cropped hair and gave him a kiss on the forehead. He smiled noticeably.

As Rachel left, she turned the lights down and closed the door. Preacher John sighed deeply. He had never felt this weak in his entire life. He was comforted by the fact that he would be beyond this world soon. Hopefully, he would see his wife and son again. His eyes closed, and he drifted off to sleep courtesy of the powerful painkillers the doctor had given him through his IV.

Preacher John woke to movement in his room. He wasn't sure how long he'd been out, so he assumed it was a nurse checking up on him. He opened his eyes and found a person standing next to his bed. A soldier, in full desert camo fatigues and a helmet covering his face.

"How do you feel, dad?" came the voice of his son Tim.

"Tim?" he asked weakly. "My boy, are you here to take me home?" There was some excitement to his soft voice.

"No, dad, I'm here to tell you to fight."

"I don't have any fight left, son. I want to see you and your mother again. It hurts too much to be away from you."

"I know, dad. I know it hurts, but it's like you always told me when I was playing football. 'You gotta work through the pain.' There is still so much for you to do on this Earth."

"I've done what I could. I spread the Word. I was a father and a husband." Preacher John tried to focus on the figure through the strong medicine.

"You're not done, dad. You've got to keep spreading the Word. You've got to be there for your family. They love you. Aunt Rachel just got you back in her life. You've got nieces and nephews to coach. A congregation to encourage. No, dad, this world isn't done with you."

Preacher John smiled and softly replied, "You would have been a great Preacher, son. But you can't change biology. I can feel the pull of death. My time is near."

"What if it wasn't, dad? Have you prayed? Have you prayed to be used by God a little longer? Or have you wanted to be reunited with us so badly that you welcomed death?"

Preacher John was silent. "You're right, son. I've been selfish. I just miss you guys so much. But if I had more time, I would use it. Help as many people as I could."

"Then pray, dad. And wait for your answer. Even if it's not the one you want."

"I will, Tim. I promise."

"No time like the present."

Preacher John smiled and closed his eyes. He began to pray silently and soon the medicine caused him to drift off. He dreamed of his family, both living and not. And for the first time in many months, he dreamed of the future.

He awoke to the sound of the nurse in his room. Sunlight streamed through the window. He wasn't sure how much of what had happened was real and what was a dream, but he knew one thing: He wasn't done with this world yet.

"Nurse," he asked weakly. "Could you set me up?"

"Absolutely," she replied. "Feelin' better today, huh?" She pushed the button on the bed controller and his head and shoulders slowly raised so he could see outside. "By the way, Preacher John, the doctor will be in soon. I hate to say it, but it's a different one than yesterday."

Preacher John replied, "No problem. I'm sure he's great." His ever-present smile, absent for weeks, had returned.

The doctor came in reading his chart. "Preacher John is it?"

"That's me, doc," he said, his voice more upbeat but still weak.

The nurse finished up and left the room. The doctor moved to the door and gently closed it behind her. He pulled up a stool next to Preacher John.

"PREACHER John, huh? So, you're a religious man, I take it?"

"More and more every day, doc," Preacher John beamed.

"Good to know. I'm a Believer myself. Say, it says you're from Redmond, OR. Do you know Sargent Francine Connelly?"

"You kiddin' me? Frankie's like a daughter to me."

"Small world, huh? I treated her in Iraq after her accident. We've been reconnecting lately. In fact, I just spoke with her last night. She's an amazing woman."

"No arguments here, doc."

"Oh, where are my manners?" He stuck out his hand. "I'm Major Lawrence Spence, but please call me Larry."

"Nice to meet you, Larry. Any friend of Frankie's is a friend of mine."

"Tell me, Preacher John would you mind if I said a small prayer for you?" Larry said, a smile forming on his face.

Epilogue #2 – Clyde's Story

Clyde sat in the dark of his living room. Little Frankie and Timmy were in her bedroom, sound asleep. Preacher John was an absolute wreck, fitfully sleeping on the couch across the room.

In Clyde's right hand were two 5.56 NATO bullet casings. Each round had struck and killed an enemy soldier in Vietnam. They were the last two rounds he fired. After the war, he vowed he would never fire another gun. Though he had killed many more enemy soldiers during his tour, he had kept these last two casings to remind him of that vow. He stared at them, squeezed them like stress balls, and shifted them around.

One month ago, someone broke into the church building and killed his beloved wife Cindy and Preacher John's wife Stella. They were good women who were probably trying to help someone who killed them for their kindness.

Clyde worried about their kids, growing up without mothers. He worried about his ability to be a good father without the love of his life. He worried if Preacher John would even survive it. He hadn't wept a single tear yet. He was too mad. Mad with worry.

The only thing Clyde could do was react. The police were no help. There were no clues, no witnesses, they said. Clyde knew different.

Across the street was a terrible old man named Singer. He was a legend in town. He hated cops. He hated religion. He hated black folks the most. "Bad enough I can hear them singin' across the street, but they sing those dumb slave songs," he was heard saying many times.

Clyde knew Singer hadn't done the crime. He was a big talker, but too old and too cowardly to actually do anything. And though he was hateful, he had no history of violence. But Singer was also the

203

biggest busybody around. Anyone who had ever gotten within half a block of his front porch had felt his icy stare.

Of course, Clyde had told the police about Singer. They visited him, and he was, predictably, uncooperative. Clyde had spent the last few weeks figuring out what to do as he took care of the kids and Preacher John. Tonight, he would react.

Quietly, he walked outside and into his garage. Grabbing some old dark blue coveralls from a hook on the wall, he slipped them on over his clothes and grabbed his work boots from a shelf. He used a ladder to climb up to the rafters and pulled an old Army footlocker down. Sitting it on his workbench, he fished his keyring out and found the old key to unlock it. He picked the lid up and the thick dust rolled off it, becoming a large plume when it hit the ground.

He reached inside and pulled out a long, oily cloth roll. He unrolled it to reveal an M-16. He pulled out a box of cleaning supplies and laid them all out on the workbench. Within minutes, he had stripped down, cleaned and reassembled the weapon. Some things you never forget, he thought.

Next, he pulled out his Colt 1911 sidearm and stripped and cleaned it, as well. This weapon had saved him several times when the Viet Cong had overrun their position. Finally, he removed his Kabar knife. He spent twenty minutes sharpening its two sides.

The battle belt inside still fit him. The pistol and knife were placed in their designated spots on the belt. He loaded the magazines with brand new rounds he had purchased earlier that day and put them in pouches on the belt. He slung the M-16 on his back and left the garage.

Singers' house was only a few blocks away. He moved quickly and quietly through alleys and yards until he stood outside his back door. He saw Singer sitting at his kitchen table, working on a plastic model of a classic car.

Clyde pulled a ski mask from his back pocket and put it on. He walked up to the back door and kicked hard, sending the thin door exploding inward. Singer fell back in his chair and scrambled along the floor. Clyde grabbed him by his shirt collar and threw him onto his couch.

"You saw who killed the women in the church. Tell me everything you saw."

"What the heck are you talkin' about? I didn't see nuttin'," Singer spat back defiantly.

Clyde pulled out his Kabar and slammed it hard into Singers' bare foot, pinning it to the floor. Singer screamed loudly.

"Tell me!" Clyde screamed.

"There was two of 'em," Singer whined, grasping at his foot. Singer spent several minutes describing their appearance through waves of pain. When he was finished, Clyde pulled the knife from his foot and turned to leave.

"Wait! Wait," Singer said. "What those boys did, well, it wasn't right. I may not like 'em, but I've had trouble sleepin'." He paused, looking at his bleeding foot. "I saw them again yesterday. They were out at that crap motel north of town. They was just sittin' on a bench, smokin'. They're probably stayin' there. You go get 'em. I won't say nuttin'."

Clyde turned again and started out the door. When he was out of sight, Singer whispered, "You kill 'em, Clyde."

Clyde made his way back home to get his car. He knew he should take the time to do some recon, think out his plan of attack. He also knew that if he thought about it too much, he wouldn't act. What he was doing was not right. Not in the eyes of God and not in

205

the eyes of his dead wife. But he was doing this for Frankie, for Timmy and for Preacher John. They needed to know peace.

He drove through the residential area of town. It was a very quiet night. His old truck made a lot of noise, but there was no one around to notice. He had stuck his gear in a sack and placed it in the floorboard just in case he got pulled over.

The Stop-Inn was a well-known shady place. At one time, it was a beautiful motor lodge common in the 1950's. Now, you could rent a room by the hour and paid extra if you wanted clean sheets. A lot of drug dealers held up there. Prostitution was common. You didn't go there unless you were looking for trouble or running from it. This was the first time Clyde had even driven by it in years.

He parked his truck half a mile away behind an old gas station. He walked through tall grass and some scattered trees until he was right across the street. He took out his binoculars and scoped the area. Sure enough, there were two men sitting on a bench smoking. One had long brown hair and beard with a denim vest. The other was very tall, bald and wore combat boots. Exactly how Singer had described them.

Clyde had no scope on his M-16, so he couldn't shoot them from far away. Truth be told, he was better with the pistol, but the M-16 was an automatic. He could spray bullets at them from close range and easily hit them dozens of times. Either way, he needed to get closer.

Suddenly, the tall man stood up and stretched. He said something to his compatriot and started walking across the street toward Clyde. Clyde knew they couldn't see him in the trees, but he was puzzled. The tall man entered the thicket of tall grass and trees ten feet away from Clyde and walked another twenty feet, stopping at a fallen tree.

The tall man bent beside the tree and opened a large cardboard box Clyde hadn't seen there. He slipped a little closer and could see the man looking through the box for something. It took an extra couple of seconds for him to realize it was one of the boxes from the Church pantry, where the ladies had been working when they were killed. They had obviously stashed the stolen goods across the street, so they wouldn't be caught with them.

Clyde was furious but took a few deep breaths and calmed down. He took out his Kabar and continued toward the tall man, whose back was to him. As he reached his target, he heard the tall man say, "Shoot man, no more Twinkies" and dropped the box in disgust.

The tall man turned and came face to face with Clyde. In one swift move, Clyde slashed the tall man's throat, slinging blood in a long trail as he did. The tall man tried to cry out but only made a gurgling sound and grabbed at his throat. He fell to the ground and Clyde stared as he shook. In less than two minutes, the tall man was dead, his blood soaking into the dirt.

Clyde bent down and stared into the man's open eyes. He hadn't bothered to put the ski mask back on yet and wanted his image burned into the man's soul as it departed his body for Hell.

Five minutes later, he was back to his observation area. He hoped 'vest man' would eventually come looking for the tall man. Soon, he felt rewarded when that very scenario took place. After nearly half an hour, vest man stood, dropped his cigarette butt and stubbed it out. Shaking his head, he started across the road toward the spot his friend entered the grassy area.

As vest man closed in on where the body lay, Clyde silently cursed himself for not moving it. If he saw the body on the ground, he might turn and run immediately, and Clyde would have to shoot him, drawing attention from the motel.

As vest man approached, he slowed but did not stop. "Dave?" he asked, unsure of what he was looking at. Clyde was silently coming up behind him when he stepped on a crumpled-up Twinkie wrapper. Vest man spun just as Clyde was stabbing downward. He instinctively put his arm up to block and the knife stabbed through his forearm. When the forearm twisted, it pulled from Clyde's grasp.

Vest man kicked Clyde, causing both men to fall backwards away from each other. He was moaning and cursing as he stood. Clyde jumped back to his feet and pulled his 1911. Vest man raised his hands in the air as blood poured down his arm.

"Come on man, I don't have any money!" Vest man coughed out. "I don't have anything worth takin'!"

"Back up!" Clyde instructed. "Put your back against the tree, now!"

"Ok, ok, man. Take it easy," vest man said backing up until he hit the fallen tree. "Now what?" he spat, with a growing defiance.

"Now I shoot you in the head and dig the bullet out of the tree," Clyde said calmly.

"Wh-what?" vest man asked, not fully comprehending.

Clyde followed through with his threat. Vest man fell to the ground, unrecognizable. Clyde bent and pulled the Kabar from his forearm, an audible slurping sound peeling off into the night. He inspected the tree with a flashlight and found the bullet lodged a couple of inches into the bark. Using the knife, he dug the lead slug out and put it into his pocket. The bullet casing was a few feet away and he retrieved it and put that in his pocket, too. He took one last look at the two bodies, then picked up the cardboard box and made his way back to the truck.

Once he was home, he left the cardboard box in the back of his truck. It wasn't uncommon for him to have boxes in his line of work. He carried his gear into the garage. His rifle and pistol were once again stripped and cleaned, then wrapped in their cloth towels and put back into the footlocker. The Kabar was thoroughly cleaned with gasoline, then sharpened again. He wrapped it and placed it in the footlocker. He went through the battle belt and pulled out all of the magazines and tools and put them in the footlocker, too. Then he closed the lid, locked it and put it back in the rafters.

The coveralls he had been wearing were removed along with his gloves and ski mask. He cleaned his boots thoroughly with gasoline, then removed several of the treads from the bottom of the soles and walked around in the dirt for a few minutes.

Clyde pulled the lead slug from the coverall's pocket. He stared at it intensely for a moment, then cleaned it thoroughly with gasoline. He walked over to his vice and placed the slug between the its jaws. Grabbing the handle, he twisted it until the slug began to flatten out. He twisted the slug and flattened it out some more. He gazed at it again. It just looked like a normal lump of lead. He tossed it onto his workbench, where it would sit for many years. The casing went in his front jeans pocket where he kept the other two from the war.

In the backyard, he went to the firepit he had built last year. He put the coveralls, gloves and ski mask in the pit, poured lighter fluid on top and lit them. The fire burned hot for several minutes, then he added some wood and took a seat, staring at the flames.

"What did you do, Clyde?" came the deep voice Clyde knew well.

"How long have you been standing there?" Clyde asked.

"Long enough to see a man cleaning up his tracks," Preacher John replied, stepping closer to the fire.

209

"I did what needed to be done," Clyde stated.

Preacher John sat next to his friend on the wooden bench. "I need the details, Clyde."

Clyde told him everything. He left nothing out. It took him nearly a half hour before he was done.

"Sounds like you covered your bases. Took the bullet so it couldn't be traced. Took the box so it couldn't be connected to the church. The police will probably chalk it up to drug activity," Preacher John suggested. "Why did you save the boots?"

"The only trace of who did it would be boot prints. Boots are hard to dispose of. The rubber sole would melt, but not burn. Finding two rubber globs in my fire pit would be suspicious. So, I changed the tread pattern a little, then scuffed them up to look like they had been that way for a while. The gasoline removed any blood that may have gotten on them."

"That's smart thinking."

"I guess," Clyde said. The two men sat in silence for a while, then Clyde began to break down.

"What did I do, John?" he said through sobs. "The things I did in Vietnam, I did for my country. I can live with that. But I never wanted to kill another man. I'm not sure God can forgive me."

Preacher John hugged his friend tight. "You did what men have been doing since the beginning. You did what was best. You defended everyone else's wives and mothers. God will forgive you because you'll ask Him too. And you'll mean it."

"I hope you're right," Clyde said weakly.

Preacher John continued to hug his friend tight as he wept. He knew Clyde had done this not only for Frankie but for he and Tim as well. He could never repay Clyde except to never bring it up again. And he vowed that if anyone ever found out, he would take the blame before Clyde could. It was the least he could do.

Epilogue #3 – Mara and Rusty continued

Rusty hated flying. He knew it was the safest form of travel. He knew Mara was an excellent pilot and had been so for almost a hundred years. Even if they crashed, he knew he wouldn't be dead long. Still, he just hated it and couldn't explain why.

"We should be in Detroit in an hour or so. Got the autopilot locked in," Mara said, emerging from the front cabin.

"Is it safe for you to be back here?" Rusty asked.

"Rusty, I take naps back here while flying cross country. The autopilot is state of the art. Besides, I'm three steps from the cockpit should anything happen."

"I know, I know," Rusty agreed. "So, tell me, why did the Sons of Aaron move to Detroit? Last I heard, they were in Greece."

"We still have offices around the world, but the main office moved to Detroit about ten years ago. There has been a lot of activity in the United States in the last three years. Detroit seemed like a good location plus the real estate is cheap. They bought a large building and retrofitted everything for a fraction of the cost of building."

"You'll have to fill me in on some of this activity," he said, taking a sip of wine to calm his nerves. "But first, tell me, what have you been working on?"

Mara smiled. "Me? Well, you're gonna love this one since you're such a technology fan. I've been studying computer technology for the last couple of decades and experimenting with new programming."

"Sounds exciting, my friend," Rusty said, tipping his glass to her.

"Don't be a smart aleck, Lazarus. For a 2,000-year-old Jew, you do sarcasm worse than a Klingon. Anyway, during some routine monitoring of the internet, I noticed someone had been making inquiries about the Sons of Aaron. Not by name, but by reputation. And I'll tell you, this guy was good. In some instances, five hundred inquiries an hour."

"Is that fast?" Rusty asked.

"Way too fast for a human. I assumed the guy was using software to perform the searches."

"And was he?"

"Of a sort. I contacted the guy through a forum and we spoke a lot over a few weeks' time. Then we Skyped—"

"Mara! I don't want to know about--"

"Skyping is like teleconferencing, you old prude. And it turned out the guy was a girl. But when I analyzed the video, I found it was completely computer generated."

"Sounds like a stalker maybe?"

"No, we got very close and she invited me to visit her in Oregon. A little town called Redmond. She was intrigued about the Sons of Aaron and wanted to help us, but I had to come to her. So, I did."

"And? Was it a 30-year-old man living in his mother's basement?"

"Well, it was a shed, but it wasn't a 30-year-old man. It was artificial intelligence. She was a Personal Digital Assistant whose programming was decades beyond anything I have ever seen."

"Amazing! And who programmed her. Is it a 'her'?"

"She identifies as a female. A teenager, really. Her programmer is another extraordinary person that wasn't even on our radar. When I visited, the programmer, Frankie, was away on a gambling trip."

"A gambling trip? Our computer genius is a gambler?"

"It's not what you think. She gambles and wins money, then funnels it through her dad's thrift store. He uses the money to help his townsfolk, she uses it to fund research. He has no idea what she is doing."

"She must be a very good gambler," Rusty noted.

"She is incredible, Rusty. She was injured in Iraq and the injuries to her brain made her amazingly intelligent. Her capacity for learning is off the charts AND she can apply what she learns. I listened to an original piano concerto she composed after listening to popular piano concertos by Brahms, Tchaikovsky, Rachmaninov and a few others. And, get this, she learned to play the piano in two hours."

"And she was not a Vessel?"

"Nope, I gave her the test before I left. I used one of the ancient prints and asked her to appraise it. No angels or demons came forward. She's just a regular person who developed an extraordinary ability."

"So, what happened with your computer friend?"

"We spoke for hours. Oddly enough, I shared everything with her and she asked how she could help. I told her we could use her help in the organization and she volunteered."

"How did her programmer take it?"

"That's the beauty of it. At her suggestion, I made a complete copy of her. Not only her core programming but everything that made up her personality. See that big suitcase over in the corner?" She pointed to a hard case with a cable running to an outlet on the wall.

"She's in there?"

"That suitcase has her entire program on it and when we get back to headquarters, I'm going to upload her onto the server. She will help us immensely."

"Won't her programmer be mad that you copied her program? That's her work."

"She doesn't know. The AI in the shed doesn't even know. She had me remove any memory of our meeting. She thought it would be easier that way."

"Amazing," Rusty said.

"Amazing was scrounging together the parts for that suitcase before her programmer came home. Luckily, the AI found them for me through local online stores. I bet I bought every hard drive for twenty miles."

"Tell me, does she have a name? This AI?"

"Pippa. Her name is Pippa."

About the Author

Robert Whitbey grew up in Shafter, CA. He attended California State University, Bakersfield, the University of Wyoming and Point Loma University. He has been a high school science teacher for over a decade and an adjunct college professor for half that time. Prior to that he spent many years working in agricultural research. His hobbies include reading, writing, gardening and golf.

He has published three prior books. His first, *How to Become a Reluctant Prepper and Why it's OK to be One*, is published under his pen name, The Reluctant Prepper. His second book and first novel, *The Angel,* is a superhero fantasy novel based in California's Central Valley. *The Vessel* continues the Small Town Heroes series on Laramie, WY.

His favorite modern authors are Peter Clines, DJ Molle and Mark Tufo.

Rob currently resides in Bakersfield, CA with his wife, Lacy, and their two sons, Dylan and Jack.

Please visit the Small Town Heroes Facebook page for more info or to contact the author. Questions are always welcome.